Marrying Chrissy

Brides of Clearwater Book 3

Melanie D. Snitker

Marrying Chrissy
(Brides of Clearwater Book 3)
© 2018 Melanie D. Snitker

Published by
Dallionz Media, LLC
P.O. Box 643
Boerne, TX 78006

Cover Image: Jennifer Pitts Photography
https://www.jenniferpittsphotography.com/

Cover: Blue Valley Author Services
http://www.bluevalleyauthorservices.com/

For permission requests, please contact the author at the e-mail below or through her website.

Melanie D. Snitker
melaniedsnitker@gmail.com
www.melaniedsnitker.com

ISBN-13: 978-1-7327432-0-5
ISBN-10: 1-7327432-0-7

Chapter One

Chrissy Laughlin ran a brush through her shoulder-length hair another time or two and then studied her reflection in the bathroom mirror. It was weird to see the dark brown strands in place of the gothic black she'd been sporting for a while. She couldn't give up the colorful purple hair segments, though. At least not until she was ready to transform them into blue or pink. A light-colored strand of hair caught her attention. Convinced that thirty-two was way too young to be getting gray hair, Chrissy grabbed hold and yanked it out with a measure of satisfaction.

She set the brush on the counter, dried her hands off on the towel—her nails painted purple to match her hair—and vacated the bathroom she shared with her mom and sister.

"It's about time," Emma, Chrissy's younger

sister, said with a frown. "I'm leaving in fifteen minutes, and I still need to brush my teeth." Emma worked for a local veterinary clinic where she managed the front desk. Instead of wearing her normal set of brightly-colored scrubs, Emma was dressed in a black, shin-length skirt and a pretty blouse.

Chrissy blinked at her. "You're sure dressed up today. Where are you going?"

"I have a job interview this morning." Emma shot her a look that said she didn't want to talk about it.

Chrissy ignored it completely. "I thought we discussed this. You can't afford to take on a second job. It's going to stress you out, and the doctor said you needed to avoid that as much as possible." It seemed like all Chrissy and their mom did was continuously try to get Emma to ease up on her schedule. Emma's heart transplant had only been a year ago, but it had drastically changed all their lives, and Emma's most of all.

Emma glanced down the hall and lowered her voice. "You know as well as I do that I've got to get more money coming in. You and Mom are great, but Mom doesn't need to take on a second job in her sixties. And neither do you. This job has potential. It pays more than what I'm making now. If I can convince them to make it full-time, I can quit working at the clinic." Her eyes misted as she blinked away the tears. Working at the vet clinic had been a dream come true for her, and it'd been heart-wrenching enough to have to go from working with animals to manning the front desk. "You two have gone above and beyond. You shouldn't have to be saddled with my medical bills forever."

Just the cost of Emma's anti-rejection medications alone had been staggering, much less the bills from the surgery itself or the treatments before she'd gotten the transplant.

They'd all decided to buy a three-bedroom house together a few years ago when Emma started to get really sick. It'd proven to be one way to save as much money as they could. Unfortunately, all their money went to paying normal house bills along with the medical stuff. They'd struggled to make ends meet the last couple of months.

Living together meant they were experts at supporting each other and irritating the snot out of each other as well.

Chrissy shook her head. "We'll figure it out, Emma. We always do."

"And part of that is my taking this job interview." She glanced at her watch. "Now I have eleven minutes." She raised an eyebrow and ducked inside the bathroom, closing the door behind her.

Chrissy sighed and headed for the kitchen. Mom looked up from her cup of coffee and slice of cinnamon raisin bread. "You are beautiful, Chrissy. I'd forgotten what you looked like without black hair." Years ago, she'd protested Chrissy's decision to dye her hair black but had since gotten used to it.

"Me, too. Thanks, Mom." Chrissy poured herself a glass of orange juice and sat down at the table. "Have you tried talking to Emma?"

"Yes, and she won't hear me out." Mom frowned. There were lines around the corners of her eyes that hadn't existed two years ago. Truthfully, Emma's illness had had a profound impact on all of them. "You know your sister. Stubborn as the day is long."

"Gee, I wonder where she got that?" Chrissy fought back a smile.

Mom gave her an amused look. "I'm surprised I have any stubbornness left after giving so much of it to the two of you." She reached over and squeezed Chrissy's hand.

Chrissy couldn't argue with her there. The three of them all tended to be incredibly pig-headed, which made for some interesting family discussions that sometimes bordered on arguments. The three of them worked well together, for the most part, which is why they'd been able to weather so many challenges lately. "Seriously, though, what are we going to do about Emma?"

"Nothing may come of this job interview. There's no sense in poking the bear for no reason. We pray, and we wait." She ate the last two bites of her bread. "You'd better head out of here. Try not to worry about your sister today."

That was much easier said than done. Mornings were always chaotic as the three of them got ready—

Emma for her job at the vet clinic, Mom for work at the bank where she'd been a teller for twenty years, and Chrissy for her managerial position at Clearwater Coffee. With two cars to share between them, Chrissy usually took one, thanks to her schedule, and then Mom and Emma took turns dropping each other off.

Chrissy arrived at Clearwater Coffee just before six in the morning. She tried to push worried thoughts of Emma aside. Emma had received excellent health reports from her doctor the last two visits. Chrissy knew she had to let go and let God look after her sister, but that was so much easier said than done. Especially when the image of her sister in the hospital, pale and nearly lifeless, still haunted Chrissy's dreams.

The sound of the bell over the coffee shop's entrance jolted Chrissy from her thoughts. She caught the door as a customer left the building before walking inside herself.

The place bustled with activity like it did every morning. People were set up at the tables, laptops open and cups of steaming coffee at their elbows. The sound of the blender and cappuccino machines filled the air.

Chrissy rounded the counter, grabbed an apron from the back, and jumped right in. Nina, one of the employees, glanced at her and then did a double take.

"Girl! What did you do to your hair? It looks fantastic."

Chrissy resisted the urge to reach up and touch it. "Thanks. I guess I was ready for a change." She shrugged. It really wasn't that big of a deal. She changed the color of portions of her hair every three to four months or so. But with money getting even tighter, going back to a more natural look was necessary.

"Well, it suits you."

Chrissy and Nina worked side by side for an hour before customer traffic slowed down enough for a breather.

Nina slumped against a counter. "You'd think we were the only coffee shop in Clearwater."

The small town of Clearwater, Texas, had a large number of coffee shops, but the prime location right on the town square made Clearwater Coffee one of the local favorites. Besides, now that the July temperatures were only rising, everyone looked for an excuse to step indoors and enjoy the air conditioning. Iced coffees were a frequently requested beverage.

The bell above the door rang as another customer came inside. Chrissy shooed Nina away. "Go take your break. I've got this one."

Nina smiled appreciatively and went to sit down with a muffin and her cell phone.

Chrissy watched as Wyatt approached the counter. A frequent customer, Wyatt was all business. He typically came inside, ordered the same thing, and was on his way again. They often exchanged pleasantries and the occasional joke, but Chrissy didn't think she'd ever seen him take a seat and relax.

He was speaking on a phone as he approached her, which happened to be one of Chrissy's pet peeves.

In fact, she made a point of never placing an order until she was off the phone. It seemed like the polite thing to do.

Wyatt used his shoulder to keep the phone against his ear. With one hand, he took his wallet out. With the other, he grabbed a chocolate bar off a display on the counter. "Yes, I realize that. I'm going to be there. I'm bringing a gift, and I've already talked to Violet about pitching in for the flowers." When he really looked at Chrissy for the first time since he entered, his eyes widened a little. He pointed to her hair and gave her a thumbs-up. Someone on the other end of the line must have said something because he sighed a little. "I don't know what you want me to do about it."

He noticed her change in hair? That surprised Chrissy, since he usually just breezed in and out of the coffee shop without lingering. You'd have to be dead not to notice him with those bright green eyes, sandy brown hair, and biceps that looked like they might split a t-shirt if he flexed his arms.

Chrissy mentally shook the image from her head and focused on her job. Wyatt lowered the phone and whispered his usual order. Chrissy nodded, added up his total, and accepted the cash he offered.

He was still talking on the phone when he moved away to wait.

Chrissy started on his coffee, thankful for the distraction. Not only from thinking about his muscular arms, but also about the financial mess waiting for her at home. Emma was probably in the middle of her interview right now. She wanted to wish her sister good luck, but only if the job would replace the one she had now. *I don't even know what to pray for, God. All I want is for Emma to stay healthy.*

She finished Wyatt's coffee, put the lid on it, and moved to the counter to hand it to him. Good grief, the guy was still on the phone. Now he looked frustrated, a frown tugging at the corners of his mouth.

"Mom, this really seems overboard." He reached for the coffee, and as his hand closed around the cup, his fingers rested on top of Chrissy's. Wyatt looked at her face, and his eyes lit up. "You know what? I'll bring a date if it means you and Dad stay off my case and let Gran enjoy her night. Yeah." His gaze went to Chrissy's name tag. "Her name's Chrissy. Of course I'm not bringing a total stranger. We've known each other for months." Wyatt winked at her.

Chrissy's jaw dropped. What? Surely he was joking. Only then did she realize they were both still holding onto his coffee cup. Suddenly, the feel of his fingers on hers had her heart rate shooting through the roof. She jerked her hand away as though some of the hot beverage had spilled over the side.

She busied herself cleaning the counters and expected Wyatt to fly out of the shop like he normally did. Instead, he finished his phone conversation, hung up, and then turned to look at her.

With a serious expression on his handsome face, he opened his mouth and asked the last question

Chrissy ever expected.

"How would you like to go with me to my grandmother's 90th birthday party?"

~*~

As soon as the words left Wyatt Tabor's lips, he wanted to take them back. Okay, maybe that wasn't the whole truth. More like he wished he wanted to take them back. As it was, he had four days before Gran's birthday, which wasn't a whole lot of time to drum up a date he didn't know he needed until five minutes ago. Of course, it'd be easier if his family would simply quit treating his lack of a love life like public property.

The way Chrissy was staring at him with her pretty light brown eyes, it was clear she had no idea what to think of his question. Finally, she looked around the room. "Are we on camera? You're trying to prank me or something, right?"

Wyatt smiled. "No cameras." He observed Chrissy for a moment and admired the combination of her short stature, colorful streaks of hair, and a smile that seemed to always brighten his day. She was adorable—he'd always thought so. He avoided the dating scene like the plague, but if it were his thing, he'd be interested in asking Chrissy out. Still, he wasn't sure what Gran would think if he walked into her birthday party with a date who had purple streaks in her hair. Not to mention the brightly-painted nails, rings on every finger, and the tattoo on her wrist.

He'd noticed the tattoo months ago. It was a vine that encircled her wrist with two tiny heart-shaped flower buds and one bloomed rose along it. He wondered more than once about the significance of the ink.

No, this wasn't Gran's ideal date for Wyatt. It wasn't Mom or Dad's, either, which did make the idea even more alluring. On the other hand, it was either bring Chrissy, or show up with no date at all. He wasn't going to win either way, but at least going with Chrissy would change things up a little.

Chrissy must have found her voice because she cleared her throat and crossed her arms. "You've known me for months?" She gave him a firm look that dared him to clarify his words.

"Technically, it's true. I've been coming in for coffee ever since someone recommended this place to me before Christmas."

"Ordering coffee from me several times a week doesn't mean you know me." Her hands moved to her hips. "Don't you have a girlfriend you could ask? Or a coworker?"

She seemed to realize the ridiculousness of her question. He wouldn't be asking his coffee barista if he had an alternative.

He could never understand why Mom had to be so obsessed with his love life. He'd been open to the possibilities of falling in love and living happily ever after. He'd even tried it once. He'd met someone he was crazy about, thought he'd fallen in love, done all the right things, and gotten engaged. And for what? To have his heart stomped into the ground. One would think that, after seeing their son dumped over money, his parents would have a little sympathy and give him some space. Instead, Mom insisted that all Gran wanted for her birthday was to see Wyatt find a girl to spend the rest of his life with. While that might be partially true, he wasn't stupid. She and Dad had other motives, and it had nothing to do with Gran's happiness.

The last thing he wanted, though, was for there to be drama on his grandmother's 90th birthday. If bringing a date to the party made Gran happy and kept his parents from broaching the subject in front of the rest of the family, it'd be worth it.

Chrissy had always come across as a nice, caring person, and he had a short timeline. He couldn't think of anyone better to ask. "It's a long story. Give me a chance to explain it to you." He glanced at the clock on the wall. "I've got to run. What time are you off work?"

"Four." The moment the word was out, she pressed her lips together.

"I'll be back then so we can talk." Wyatt took a sip of his coffee. Perfect as always. She opened her mouth to object, but he held up a finger, smiled, and said, "I'll see you then. Have a great day."

With a wave over his shoulder, he left the cool air of the coffee shop and stepped into the sweltering July heat. These were the times when he wished he could stomach iced coffee. He'd tried it once or twice, but coffee was meant to be hot. Even if it seemed silly to drink a cup of it when temps were nearing one hundred, Wyatt could admit he was addicted to the caffeine fix.

Once in his vehicle, he drove to the other side of town to the Clearwater Country Club that was less than a mile from the Guadalupe River. His parents, Ben and Elise Tabor, had owned the club for years, and his grandparents before that. It'd grown from a little eighteen-hole golf course to the kind of establishment where large businesses brought their potential clients out to woo them. Between the day spa, stables, and renowned five-star restaurant on the grounds, the club had landed itself in more than one travel magazine as a worthwhile destination.

The success of the place made it easy for his dad to save up and provide more for his family than he'd ever thought possible. Wyatt and his three sisters grew up wanting for nothing. At the same time, their dad insisted that they also learn to work and appreciate what they had. While he set aside a share of the family's wealth for each of them, their money was put into individual bank accounts that were only accessible after their twenty-first birthdays.

Violet had managed to ruin that for the rest of them. As the oldest in the family by five years, she'd taken her money, gone on a tour of the world, and come back nearly broke two years later. She'd spent the last fifteen years married to a man that didn't have nearly as much money as she'd like him to have and made sure her unhappiness with life was evident to the rest of the family.

Their father had since decided to hold onto their inheritance until he was satisfied that they were well established in life. With the influence of their mother, unfortunately, that meant seeing their children happily married and settled in Clearwater. Lucy, his other older sister, was married. The only ones left waiting for the blessing of their parents—and ultimately their inheritance—were Wyatt and Bonnie.

When Wyatt graduated college with a degree in business, Dad made him a manager of the country club. Over the years, that position morphed into being a business partner and head of personnel. In other words, he picked up the slack where needed.

He normally didn't mind, but it irritated Wyatt to no end that his dedication didn't seem to be enough to earn his inheritance. Unfortunately, he'd made the mistake of sharing his future business goals with his father.

It was Wyatt's dream to open Joyful Hope Stables, a place where people could enjoy horses and learn how to ride at prices anyone could afford. He got the idea from the few horses they had at the country club. Wyatt had witnessed the way the horses helped people gain self-confidence, including Gran, and wanted to extend that to others. Maybe even hire some therapists to provide hippotherapy to adults and children alike.

It was a goal his father found ludicrous, insisting that putting money into a charity project that would never earn it back was foolhardy. Wyatt had long ago stopped trying to explain his dreams. While he got along with his father okay, they would never see eye to eye when it came to managing money.

Mom explained that until Dad was convinced that Wyatt was settled and stable, he'd see none of that inheritance money.

He could've seen his dreams realized a lot earlier, but since he didn't have a family to support, he'd been putting away money every month. He was finally in reach of going forward with his plans, and all without the use of his family's money.

As Wyatt settled in his office and went through a list of resumes he was considering for a job opening in the golf center, he couldn't keep his mind off Chrissy and what he'd asked her.

If her expression was any indication, there was no way she was going to agree to go with him to Gran's birthday. He read through another resume before setting it aside. A thought came to him.

What if he offered to pay Chrissy? Hiring a woman to pose as his date to his own grandmother's birthday party wasn't too pathetic, was it?

The moment the thought went through Wyatt's mind, he dismissed it. That was a crazy idea. If his family ever found out that he'd become so desperate, they would never let him live it down. He couldn't blame them, either. He would rib one of his sisters for months over something as crazy as this.

The idea ping-ponged between the worst thing he'd come up with and one that seemed plausible as he worked his way through the day. By the time three forty-five rolled around, he was ready to put the country club behind him and go talk to Chrissy. With any luck, she'd take pity on him after hearing his story, give him one of those smiles that seemed to light up the coffee shop, and agree to go with him out of the goodness of her heart.

Hey, a guy could hope.

Chapter Two

Wyatt waited for Chrissy to hang up her apron, gather her bag, and walk around the counter. Only then did he ask her if she'd like to sit down so they could talk. To his surprise, she shook her head.

"I'm in here all day. There's only so much coffee smell a girl can take. Let's walk down to the fountain." She led the way through the dining area and outside. The heat of the day hadn't begun to diminish yet, leaving the air feeling thick with humidity.

Wyatt followed, aware of how the ends of her hair bounced around her shoulders as she moved. The sun brought out the stripes of purple, which were more visible now that her hair was a lighter color.

The fountain she spoke of was at the center of the downtown area less than a block from the coffee shop. It was a well-known fixture during town events such as antique car shows, holiday festivals, and even the chili cook-off in the fall.

Right now, most people in the area were cutting through the center on their way to or from somewhere else. Chrissy approached the fountain and sat on the circular brick rim that served as a bench. She looked at Wyatt expectantly.

He'd had everything all planned out when he left work. Now those words tumbled around inside his head like a load of socks in the dryer. He finally sat down beside her and took a deep breath. "Okay, I'm going to try and make a long story short here."

He paused. "My paternal grandmother just turned ninety, and we're celebrating with a party this weekend. I'm especially close to her. I have three sisters and no boy cousins. It's Gran's dream to see me married so that I can carry on the Tabor name and be happy." He sighed, wishing it didn't all sound quite as far-fetched as it did. "Or at least that's what my parents are constantly telling me. I'm going to be honest and say I think it's more them than it is her, but once my mom gets something in her head, there's no talking her out of it. At this point, I need to take a date to hopefully make my parents happy enough to let the subject drop. Then maybe Gran can actually enjoy her birthday and not have to witness yet another round of family drama."

Chrissy watched him warily as she ran one hand through the fountain water. The movement caused little ripples to extend from her skin in every direction.

"You're kidding."

"If someone told me this, I'd feel the same way. But I promise, I'm not joking. Gran's birthday is four days away, and I need someone to come as my date."

"So instead of actually finding a girlfriend, you're just going to pick one out at the coffee shop like you would a bagel?" Her voice rose just slightly as she spoke. She pulled her hand out of the water, wiped it off on her jeans, and then rested it on her lap. Drops of water darkened the bricks and the fabric of her pants. "You realize just how desperate that sounds, right?"

"Of course I do. That's why it's important that my family assumes you and I have known each other for a while and that you wanted to go to this party with me."

The look of disbelief on her face gave way to exasperation. "I'm sorry. I'm not in the habit of blatantly lying to strangers." She stood up and brushed off the seat of her pants. "Look, I do hope that your grandmother has a wonderful birthday."

Wyatt leapt to his feet and grabbed her wrist to keep her from walking away. "Contrary to how it might look now, I'm not in the habit of lying, either. This is the lesser of two evils. I care a great deal for Gran, and I'll do anything to make this celebration a good one for her. If that means making people happy for one night, then it's worth it. Do you get what I'm saying?" He let go of her wrist, and she took a step backward.

He could tell she was feeling sympathetic toward

him and his story. But he could also see that she hadn't been convinced. He couldn't blame her. The original plan that he'd considered over and over again back at the club came to mind. Before he could second-guess himself, he blurted out his thoughts. "What if I paid you for your trouble?"

"Excuse me?"

Chrissy's eyes widened, and this was the first time Wyatt noticed the flecks of gold amid the brown. There was something about her eyes that made him want to keep staring into them. Instead, the frown on her face, coupled with the way she'd dropped her arms and straightened her spine, told him he was losing her attention fast.

Wyatt held up a hand to stop her. "I get that this is a weird and uncomfortable situation. But if you go with me to Gran's birthday, you'll be doing me a huge favor. Essentially, you'll be my birthday gift to her. So if I pay you for your time, I'm really just buying Gran a birthday gift." He cringed at how cheesy that sounded. "Five hundred bucks for the day."

If he thought her eyes were big before...

"You're going to pay me five hundred dollars to have dinner and cake with your family? Who can afford to do that?"

He wasn't about to tell her that it didn't even make a dent in his bank account, but that wasn't going to help him out now. "The party is being hosted at the country club at five on Sunday evening. I doubt it'll last more than three hours, if that long. There will be steak, chicken, and cake and ice cream for dessert. I'll pick you up, take you home, and then we can go back to small talk at the coffee shop again. Come on, what do you say?"

~*~

Chrissy truly wanted to laugh at Wyatt, tell him no, and walk away. But five hundred dollars for one evening? That was pretty hard to pass up, especially when it would pay for most of Emma's medication for the month.

He'd mentioned that having a stranger go with him to the party and lying about knowing each other was the lesser of two evils. Maybe that was the case for her, too. Maybe it was more important to get this extra money to help Emma than it was to tell what would amount to a little lie. Not to mention that, technically, he was the one telling it anyway.

Ugh, she hated that she even had to seriously consider something like this to make extra money. Thinking about Emma going into the job interview this morning was enough to make up Chrissy's mind. *Okay, God. Is it horrible I'm even considering it? Surely You understand why I'm doing this.*

She pointed a finger at him. "Five hundred dollars, and I'm out of there by nine no matter what's going on with the party."

He seemed surprised, yet hopeful, that she might be agreeing to his crazy scheme. "Absolutely."

"And you'll pay me in cash when you pick me up?"

"I'll pay you half then and half when I drop you off at your house that evening."

Chrissy would've rather had the money all upfront but understood where he was coming from. "Okay, that's fair."

"So you'll do it?" He ran his fingers through his hair. Hair that magically fell back into place despite the humid air and the gentle breeze. He slid his hands into the pockets of his black slacks.

For the first time, Chrissy noted how fancy his button-down shirt was. Where did he work? She looked into his green eyes and the hope shining there.

"Yeah, I'll do it."

"This is great!" He pulled his cell phone from his pocket. "What's your number? I'll text you mine, and that way we can stay in touch between now and then. The party is casual, so don't feel like you need to dress up. Do you know where the country club is?"

"Yes, I do." There was no need to mention that Chrissy had driven by many times but had never actually stepped a toenail inside. She couldn't afford the membership if she'd wanted one. Against her better judgment, Chrissy gave him her cell phone number. Moments later, her own phone pinged. She glanced at the screen and the number along with the words, "Wyatt Tabor." She'd be sure to add him to her contact list once she got home. "Okay, it came through."

"Seriously, thank you. You're saving me, and if we can keep this between the two of us, I'd appreciate it."

He gave her a smile then, one that lit up his eyes and brought out a subtle dimple in his right cheek. As if he weren't already attractive enough. Unable to come up with the words anyway, Chrissy made a motion to lock her lips and throw the invisible key over her shoulder.

What she really needed to do was go home and see how Emma's interview went. "I'd better get going. Maybe I'll you later this week."

"Absolutely. Have a good evening, Chrissy."

"Yeah, you, too." They waved at each other as though they'd just stopped to visit about the weather and went their separate ways.

This was, without a doubt, one of the strangest days Chrissy had ever had.

By the time she got home, she was starving, a little grumpy from dealing with the hot weather, and more than ready to kick her tennis shoes off and watch some TV. Emma's car was already in the driveway, meaning Chrissy was the last to get home.

She unlocked the front door, stepped inside, and released a happy sigh as cool air enveloped her. Chrissy dropped her bag and keys on the nearby table and left her shoes on the floor nearby. The scents of spaghetti and garlic bread drew her to the kitchen.

Mom was draining noodles in the sink while Emma pulled a pan of garlic bread out of the oven.

They both looked up and smiled at Chrissy.

"I wasn't sure you were going to make it," Mom said. "I was just about to call and make sure everything was okay."

"I'm sorry I was late. I got held up on my way out the door." She noted Emma's casual clothes. "How'd the interview go?"

Emma shrugged. "Who can tell? I didn't completely blow it, but I don't think I aced it either. I'm supposed to hear back on Monday. I guess they have a number of other interviews scheduled this week."

Chrissy exchanged a look with Mom, who gave her a firm glare instructing her to stay quiet.

"Well, I'll be praying." Praying that God would see fit to do whatever was necessary to keep Emma healthy.

"Thanks. What about you? How was your day?" Emma placed the garlic toast on a plate and carried it over to the little round table in the middle of their tiny dining area.

Chrissy used pot holders to transport the sauce followed by Mom and the noodles. "Oh, you know. I made some coffee. Served some scones." *Accepted five hundred dollars to go on a date with a guy I barely know.* "It was a Monday."

They sat down, Mom said a prayer for their food, and they began to dish it out. Once everyone had what they needed, Mom twirled some spaghetti around her fork but didn't take the bite. "Well, it was pretty crazy at the bank today. We had a customer get so upset that the security guards had to escort him from the building."

"What?!" Chrissy quickly finished her mouthful of food. "Was he your customer?"

"Thankfully, no. But I worry about him coming back. You always hear about angry customers returning to a business to seek revenge." Mom chewed on her lower lip. The spaghetti noodles on her fork unwound themselves and flopped back onto her plate.

"I doubt you have to worry about that, Mom," Emma reassured her. "I think that mostly happens on TV. I'm sure the security guard got it taken care of, and hopefully you'll never see the guy again."

As Mom and Emma tried to remember which television show they'd seen lately that closely resembled Mom's day, Chrissy's mind wandered back to her conversation with Wyatt.

Everything about him—from his fancy shirt to the expensive shoes he wore—spoke of money. Not to mention the fact he didn't even flinch at offering half a grand to get her to go to the party with him. Here they were eating homemade spaghetti at a worn table in a crowded house. Where was Wyatt?

She pictured him in a mansion with a plate of caviar and crackers in front of him. Okay, maybe not caviar. Steak. The best cut cooked to perfection. She couldn't even remember the last time she'd eaten steak, a food that was a bit outside of their grocery budget.

There was no doubt she and Wyatt were nothing

alike. The whole "opposites attract" idea flitted into her mind, and she mentally batted it away. That didn't work in real life. She'd pose as his date at the party, and that would be it.

Suddenly, her mind began to wander as she contemplated different possibilities. Would he introduce her as his date or his girlfriend? Surely she wouldn't be expected to show any kind of affection toward him outside of sitting with him.

Chrissy's chest tightened. No longer hungry, she pushed the spaghetti around on her plate and finally laid the fork down.

A long list of questions formed in her mind— questions she should've had the good sense to ask Wyatt *before* she'd agreed to this crazy scheme of his.

"You okay, Chris?"

The sound of Mom's voice along with the touch of her hand was what finally jolted Chrissy back to the present. Both Mom and Emma were staring at her, concerned.

"Yeah, I'm fine. Sorry, just tired, I guess." She'd eventually tell them about the pseudo-date—they kept very little from each other—but she didn't have it in her tonight.

"Maybe you should turn in early," Mom suggested.

"I might do that." Chrissy did her best to eat a piece of garlic bread.

That night, Chrissy tossed and turned as different scenarios played themselves out in her dreams. Most were boring, some completely random, but it was the scenario where Wyatt put his arm around her shoulder and drew her in for a kiss that stayed with her when she woke up the next morning.

Chapter Three

Chrissy looked up from the cash register Wednesday morning and saw her friend, Raven Shaw, come into the coffee shop. "Hey! It's so good to see you. It feels like it's been forever."

Raven grinned. "You, too! I know, I'm sorry I haven't been in as much lately." She gave her coffee order and then, since there was a brief lull in customers, leaned against the counter to chat. "Heath's been helping his dad renovate the store."

That had Chrissy looking up with surprise. "You're joking."

Heath's father owned the camping and outdoor store in Clearwater. The building had been in need of some updating for a while, but he had been too stubborn to let Heath—or anyone else—help him make the changes. "How are they getting along?"

"It depends on which day you ask me." Raven laughed. "Anyway, I've been driving out that way several mornings a week, which means I haven't had enough time to stop by here before getting to work." Raven was a physical therapist at Clearwater Rehabilitation Center. That's where she and Heath reconnected when he came in for therapy after a football injury. The couple got married this past New Year's Eve.

"I totally understand, it's okay. I just miss seeing you." Chrissy put the lid on her cup of coffee. "We should meet for lunch or something next week." The bell chimed over the door, and she held up a finger when she saw it was Wyatt. "Hold just one sec."

She hadn't known what to expect the next time she saw him and worried it might be awkward. But Wyatt greeted her with a smile and a wave.

"Good morning, Chrissy."

"Good morning." She'd always thought he was attractive, but now that she knew she was going to a party with him, she found herself studying his appearance even more. His smile immediately brought out one of her own. Oh, and the way his hair fell just past his ears made her want to reach up and push it back a little. Ridiculous, right? "Your usual?" Chrissy tried to ignore the way Raven was watching them curiously. While Raven was one of her best friends, Chrissy wasn't quite ready to explain everything between her and Wyatt. Especially when not even her own mom and sister knew about this weird arrangement yet.

"That would be great. Thank you." Wyatt handed her a bill for his order and instructed her to keep the change.

She accepted the tip with a smile. He went to sit at one of the small tables while Chrissy got to work making his coffee.

Raven walked over to the counter next to her and whispered, "So, who's that?"

Chrissy shrugged. "He's a regular customer."

"Mmm-hmm." Raven took a sip of her coffee. "And the way your cheeks are turning pink tells me there's a lot more to it than that."

Chrissy cast a furtive glance in Wyatt's direction, hoping he couldn't hear any of their conversation. "It's a long story."

"One you'll have to tell me over lunch. I have to run, but I'll call so we can set something up."

"That sounds good. I'll talk to you soon."

"You, too." Raven said goodbye and left the shop.

Chrissy smiled as she thought about her friend. Raven was one of the most outspoken people she knew. If Chrissy wanted an honest opinion about anything, she could count on Raven to give her one. But the coffee shop was not the place for such a conversation, especially with Wyatt sitting right over there. In fact, she'd planned on stopping him and asking him about the public displays of affection at the birthday party. Now that he was here, though, and looking at her with those striking green eyes, the last thing she wanted to bring up was the topic of displaying affection of any kind.

Maybe she could text him later. That would work, right?

She finished preparing his coffee and handed it to him. Was it just her, or did he let his fingers linger over hers a little longer than necessary when he accepted the cup? Lovely, now she was becoming neurotic.

He smiled again and waved on his way out.

Chrissy wouldn't have admitted it to anybody, but she thought about that smile frequently throughout the eternally long day. It was a relief when she finally got off work and headed for her car. Once inside, she started the engine and cranked up the air conditioner. She pulled her phone out and started her text to Wyatt before she lost her nerve.

"Okay, so about Sunday. Is your family expecting any PDA?"

The response was almost immediate. "PDA?"

Chrissy sighed and responded, "Public displays of affection."

Seconds later, her phone rang, and Wyatt's name and number appeared. Chrissy swiped the screen with a finger. "Hello?"

"Hey. Don't worry about it. My family is large and crazy. No one's going to really notice whether we're demonstrating public displays of affection or not." There was a bit of humor in his voice. "Tell you what, if worse comes to worst and someone in my family starts to wonder, we'll limit the contact to holding hands. Does that sound agreeable?"

Not particularly. It wasn't that big of a deal, though, right? She shook people's hands all the time. Chrissy would think of it as a prolonged handshake. And at least they'd have their boundaries set before the party so there weren't any surprises. "Yes. But only if necessary."

"You got it."

Chrissy imagined him giving her a salute. "Okay. Well, I'll let you go. I'm sure you have things to do and coffee to drink." Ugh, she sounded lame. Just because he drank coffee every time she saw him didn't mean that's all he drank when he got home.

His deep chuckle filtered through the phone and washed over Chrissy. Her heart did a little flip, which she chose to ignore.

"I'll see you at five on Sunday. Bye, Chrissy."

"Goodbye."

The conversation only helped Chrissy feel a little better as she drove home. Emma looked up from her spot at the kitchen counter when Chrissy walked in.

"Oh, good. Help me chop some veggies, will you?" She slid a cutting board in Chrissy's direction and then handed her a knife. "Mom's taking a shower before dinner. She has to be at work early tomorrow for a meeting or something."

Chrissy took the knife and started chopping carrots and celery. "What are we making here?"

"Stir fry with noodles. It just sounded good." Emma added salt and pepper to the pork she was cooking. When she reached for a high-sodium seasoning, Chrissy cleared her throat which only earned her a sharp look from her sister. "Don't start with me. I need some flavor in my food tonight."

Chrissy frowned. Emma had been great with her strict diet since her heart transplant. In fact, Chrissy admired her for it. If Emma was willing to throw it all away on a random Wednesday, something must have happened. She stayed silent, though, and waited for Emma to say something first. Chrissy knew full well that pushing her sister never made a difference.

The sounds of her knife working collided with the sizzling of the meat in the skillet. It was only after they'd added the vegetables that Emma released a heavy sigh and leaned against the counter. "I didn't get the job."

"What?" Chrissy joined her, their elbows touching. "I thought they weren't going to let you know until Monday."

"Either they found the perfect employee right off, or they knew immediately I wasn't right for the position." Sarcasm dripped from her voice. "I needed that job, Chris."

"I know."

"And you're glad I didn't get it." There was no accusation there, just finality.

"I am. But only for your health, Emma. Your life is more important than how much money you're bringing in." Chrissy nudged her. "I'm serious."

"I know you are. But I hate that you and Mom are working like crazy to pay for my medical issues. It's not fair to either of you."

Shuffling noises brought their attention to Mom standing in the doorway. "I don't hear either of us complaining," she said.

Emma sniffed. "Maybe not, but it's still really messed up." When both Chrissy and Mom stuck their tongues out at her, Emma finally chuckled softly. "You two are something else, you know that?"

Mom came into the room and pulled her daughters into a hug. "Things aren't easy right now, but we've got each other's back. The important thing is we're together. We're all here and alive and healthy. Everything else is gravy."

Chrissy hadn't known when to tell them about her weird date with Wyatt, but this seemed like an opportune time. "I've got your medication covered for the month." When they both looked at her in surprise, she elaborated. "I'm being paid five hundred dollars to go on a date with a guy who frequents the coffee shop."

They stared at her as though waiting for her to start laughing. Emma's mouth opened slightly and closed again. "You're joking."

"I'm not, I promise." As they finished dinner, Chrissy told them all about the weird arrangement. Mom thought it was hilarious, while Emma teased Chrissy mercilessly.

"You just watch, Chris. You're going to go and fall in love with him. And one day, he'll tell your kids that he had to pay you to go on your first date together."

~*~

Wyatt glanced at Chrissy out of the corner of his eye. She was sitting in the passenger seat of his Jeep, her hands clasped together in her lap. He took in her jeans, scoop-neck shirt, and the way she had a bit of her hair pinned back and smiled.

She'd barely said a word since he'd picked her up from the address she'd texted to him. At the time, he couldn't help but notice the two other women watching from one of the small windows in the front of the house. A house that was not only tiny, but also in desperate need of some repairs. The paint was faded, and the minuscule yard required some attention as well.

"So, our audience. Were they related to you or just friends?"

Chrissy looked at him with a puzzled expression before it melted to a small smile. "That was my sister and my mom. They find this entire situation very amusing."

"You told them that I'm paying you?" For some reason, Wyatt had just assumed he and Chrissy were the only two people who would know about it. Had he known her family was watching, he wouldn't have just handed Chrissy half the money before opening the

Jeep's door for her. He could only imagine what they must think of him.

"I don't keep secrets from my family."

Her tone was even, but the implication was there. Clearly, he did keep secrets from his, or he wouldn't have to hire someone to go as his date in the first place. He wasn't sure which bothered him the most: that he was lying to Gran or that Chrissy might assume this was customary for him.

"I promise I'm not in the habit of hiring women to go to family functions." He swallowed. He wasn't in the habit of going out with women in general. "Gran and I have always been incredibly close. She's ninety. If the one thing she wants from me is to bring a date, and it buys peace at her party on top of it, then it was well worth the five hundred dollars." The light turned red, and Wyatt pulled to a stop. He looked at Chrissy, relieved to see there was no sign of judgment on her face, only understanding.

"Trust me. I get doing something a little outrageous for someone you're close to." She said it with her gaze fixed on something on the other side of the windshield. She was silent for several moments before she shook herself and sat up straighter. "Okay, so tell me about your family."

"I'll warn you, we have quite a bit of family in the area, but the main people I'll be introducing you to are my Gran, my parents, and my three sisters. Violet is the oldest, then Lucy, I came next, and then Bonnie is the youngest. Or the baby, as we like to tease her." The light turned green, and Wyatt continued their drive to the country club. "Lucy and Violet are married, so there will be their husbands and a combination of four kids running around." He smiled. "Just stick with me, and everything will be fine. Are you allergic to any foods or anything like that?"

She seemed surprised by his question. "No. Thanks for checking."

"Sure." He turned onto the paved drive that led down a winding road to the Clearwater Country Club. Wrought iron fencing protected the club and its grounds when the place was closed and added personality to the property. The drive led through dense trees to a large parking lot. There was a covered area as well as valet parking available. Wyatt chose a spot as close to the clubhouse as he could without taking up employee parking. As manager of the place, he usually claimed one during the week. Tonight, though, he really didn't want to explain to Chrissy how his family was connected to the country club.

He parked and caught Chrissy brushing at the jeans she wore and then pulling at the lace on her short-sleeved shirt. Wyatt laid a hand on her shoulder. "Don't even think twice. What you are wearing is great, and you look beautiful."

He wasn't sure which of them was more surprised by his words. He meant it, though. The purple shirt went nicely with the purple streaks in her hair and her matching nails. While it was still a bit different compared to what his family would expect,

36

this wasn't anywhere near as bright of a look as he'd seen Chrissy wear in the past. Even with the black hair that sported rainbow streaks, and neon fingernail polish, she'd snagged his attention. Not that he ever let her know. Noticing a woman and doing something about it were two entirely different things.

"Thank you," Chrissy said just above a whisper. "Please clue me in on things I need to know as we go, okay? And remember, I'm out of here by nine."

Wyatt stifled a smile. "Yes, I remember. Shall we?"

She nodded slightly. He got out of the car and went around to open Chrissy's door for her and then retrieved a wrapped gift from the back seat.

Chrissy gasped. "I didn't even think about that. Should I have gotten her something, too?"

Her genuine concern was sweet. He smiled. "I've got you covered. I signed both of our names to the card."

She flashed him a look of relief. "What did we get her?"

"An assortment of chocolate truffles. Trust me, she'll love them." With one hand resting lightly on Chrissy's back, he escorted her past the numerous rosebushes to the main door of the clubhouse. He felt her spine stiffen slightly as Violet greeted them before they even reached the door. "Hey, you two. You're almost late. I think everyone else is already here. Come on inside, we're on the back patio."

Violet eyed Chrissy curiously before holding out

a hand. "I'm Wyatt's oldest sister, Violet. It's nice to meet you."

To Chrissy's credit, any nervousness she'd exhibited before seemed to melt away. She shook hands with a smile. "Chrissy. It's great to meet you, too."

They followed Violet through the ornately decorated clubhouse and out the double doors to the back patio. There they found Gran surrounded by Wyatt's large family. He wondered if Chrissy was feeling overwhelmed. He knew all these people, and it was almost too much for him. He again put a protective hand on her back.

He introduced her to a variety of people as they made their way to Gran. She smiled up at him as though he were the one person she'd been waiting to see. That was Gran. She had a way of making everyone feel special and treasured. "Oh, Wyatt, I'm so glad you made it."

He ducked down, gave her a long hug, and breathed in the scent of lavender and peppermint that he'd associated with her for as long as he could remember. "As if I would miss it. Happy birthday, Gran." He placed the wrapped gift in her lap before stepping to the side so Chrissy could get closer. "This is my date, Chrissy. And this young lady here is Evelyn Tabor, my grandmother."

Gran reached for Chrissy's hand and tugged her down for a hug. She then put a hand on Chrissy's cheek. "It's wonderful to meet you, honey."

"You, too, Mrs. Tabor."

Gran chuckled. "You just call me Gran like everyone else." She smiled sweetly. "Besides, if you're dating my grandson, you're practically family."

Wyatt couldn't see Chrissy's face at that moment and wished he knew how she was reacting. But instead of Chrissy stepping away or acting flustered, she simply said, "That's so kind of you, Gran. Happy birthday."

Those few words took Wyatt's respect for Chrissy and drove it up a few notches. In that moment, he knew Chrissy would handle the evening just fine.

Gran shook the boxed gift they'd given her. "Is it okay if I open this now?"

Wyatt motioned to it. "Of course. A woman who is ninety years young should be able to open her gifts whenever she wants."

"Good answer." Gran winked at Chrissy. "Now you know why he's my favorite grandson."

"I'm your only grandson." Wyatt chuckled.

Chrissy surprised him by moving to his side, her arm brushing his, as they watched Gran open the gift. The moment she saw the large variety of chocolate truffles, she reached for one, unwrapped it, and took a bite. Her eyes closed with bliss as she let it melt in her mouth.

"My favorite." She finished the truffle before speaking again. "You know I've been fortunate enough to have two true loves in my life: my Earl, may he rest in peace…" She paused for dramatic effect. "…and chocolate truffles."

Everyone within hearing distance erupted in laughter. Amid it all, the sweet sound of Chrissy's laugh snagged his attention.

Gran obviously approved of Chrissy, something that warmed him more than it should have. Now Violet, on the other hand, was staring at them with that suspicious look in her eyes. His hope that she'd meet Chrissy and let it go evaporated.

Wyatt had to fight the instinct to put an arm around Chrissy and draw her closer. After her question about public displays of affection, he doubted she'd welcome it.

Chapter Four

There was no way Chrissy was going to remember the names of everyone she'd met so far at Gran's birthday party. Although she supposed she didn't need to, since she wasn't likely to see any of these people again after tonight.

The thought should have made her feel better, but instead, she was almost disappointed. Which was silly, right? Not that her family wasn't great; she loved her mom and sister. While they didn't see their few extended family members very often, Chrissy always enjoyed the rare occasions. But this party, where so many people gathered out of love for the family's matriarch, was touching.

What could've been an awkward event was surprisingly enjoyable. A big part of that, though, had to do with Wyatt's undivided attention. They'd gone to the party together, but she hadn't expected him to stay nearby for the entire duration. He'd asked her if she needed something to drink before she realized she was thirsty, escorted her to the line where they chose what they wanted to eat for dinner, and then sat in the chair next to her at one of the tables.

Chrissy looked around the large covered patio as people ate and visited. The area had to be larger than her entire house. Honeysuckle and climbing roses covered the white fencing along one side, and their fragrance tickled Chrissy's nose. Meanwhile, fans above kept the air flowing and chased away the Texas heat.

As fancy as the country club was, she'd half expected crystal and china. Instead, they used thick, plastic plates that were much fancier than paper. Chrissy enjoyed her New York strip steak and mashed potatoes and gravy. Although, compared to the kind of food she usually ate, this was pretty uptown all on its own. Thankfully, she seemed to blend in with the crowd.

Wyatt gently bumped her shoulder with his. When she looked at him, she found him smiling with a hint of humor in his eyes. "Earth to Chrissy. You doing okay?"

"I'm good, thanks." She drank the last of her punch. "Just people-watching. I'm usually too busy at the coffee shop to do a lot of that. It's nice to sit and be invisible for a while." He said nothing, and she glanced at him. He was watching her thoughtfully.

"What?"

"Trust me, you're never invisible."

Chrissy's hand immediately went to the purple streak in her hair, and her eyes flitted to her nails. Maybe she should've toned things down a little. Was he wishing that she had? Had someone mentioned something to him?

Before her mind could wander further, he captured her hand in his. "That's not what I'm talking about." He squeezed it gently before standing up.

Then what did he mean? She wanted him to elaborate, but he was already gathering their empty plates.

"I'm going to take these to the trash. Would you like something else to drink?"

She glanced at her cup. "Yes, please. More punch would be great."

"You've got it. I'll be back shortly."

She nodded. He gave her a smile and disappeared into the crowd. He wasn't gone a full minute before Violet slid into the seat across from Chrissy. She pushed some of her sandy brown hair out of her face and offered a friendly smile tinged with something else Chrissy couldn't quite define. It was almost as though her smile was just a little too sweet.

There was a strong resemblance between Violet, Wyatt, and the other two siblings she'd met. They all had the same-colored hair, green or hazel eyes, and the same strong nose. A big contrast to her own family, where no one ever pegged Chrissy and Emma for sisters and were later surprised when they discovered that was the case.

Violet nodded toward the crowd of happy people. "So what do you think? I hope you're having fun."

"You know, I am." It was nice to be able to say that honestly. "Everyone's been very welcoming."

"We're a pretty good bunch. Most of us, anyway." Violet folded her arms on the table and leaned forward. "The fact that Wyatt brought you here is a big deal. He doesn't do that, you know. Bring women to family functions. At least not since Ashley." She paused. "He has told you about Ashley, right?"

Chrissy tried to control her reaction to the question. No, Wyatt hadn't told her about Ashley. And why should he? They barely knew each other. Chrissy guessed Ashley must be an old girlfriend or something along those lines. She ignored the zing of jealousy as she scrambled for what to say. She wasn't about to lie, and she couldn't tell the truth, either. "I've never met Ashley, but I didn't realize he was so hesitant to bring women to family functions. I guess I should feel honored." Hopefully that answer would be good enough.

Violet leaned back in her chair then and studied Chrissy. "You certainly should. What did you say or do to convince him? Goodness knows the rest of us haven't been able to accomplish in the last five years what you have in the last..." She raised an eyebrow. "Exactly how long have you and my brother known each other?"

Did that mean Wyatt hadn't dated anyone in five years? Or had he only kept his love interests safely away from his sister? Curiosity burned until Chrissy realized Violet was still staring at her, waiting for an answer. Chrissy tried to push down the irritation that bubbled out of nowhere. Didn't Wyatt say Violet was married? Where was her husband? Or kids? Surely she had someone else she could bother.

"I met Wyatt back in December." That was the truth. Why it was bothering Chrissy so much to be accused of lying was beyond her, although her very purpose for being here was shady at best. There was something about Violet that rubbed her the wrong way. She may not know Violet well, but Chrissy could detect sibling mischievousness when she saw it. As much as she wanted to know who Ashley was, Chrissy was being baited, and she refused to bite. "Well, it's been wonderful to help Gran celebrate her birthday."

Speaking of Gran, she was sitting back in a comfy chair, happily visiting with anyone that stopped by and said hello. While the wrinkles on her face and the thin skin on her shaky hands attested to her age, her laughter and the way she seemed to enjoy life spoke of a much younger woman. Chrissy could tell Evelyn Tabor was a woman she would enjoy sitting down and visiting with.

Chrissy barely remembered her own grandmother. She'd never had the kind of close relationship that Wyatt and his sisters seemed to have with theirs. Was it wrong to envy them for it?

Wyatt returned and set Chrissy's cup down in front of her. He sat to her right and let his arm drape across the back of Chrissy's chair before fixing his sister with a curious look. "You two doing alright?"

"We're good. Just chatting." Violet seemed to take them both in. "So Wyatt, when are you going to bring Chrissy to a family dinner?"

Her question seemed to throw him, and he hesitated. "What?"

"When are you going to bring Chrissy to one of our family dinners? It'd be nice if we had a chance to get to know her in a more intimate setting." There was something about her expression and the tone of her voice that suggested she wasn't all that fond of the idea.

Wyatt looked at Chrissy and gave her a little shrug. "I don't know, Violet. After having to deal with this crazy crowd, I wouldn't blame her if she never attended another Tabor event again."

Chrissy smiled at him. "I have to admit these large gatherings overwhelm me. But it's been wonderful being welcomed by your family."

Violet didn't seem happy with Chrissy's response. Her brows drew together, and she opened her mouth to say something else when Mrs. Tabor clapped her hands to get everyone's attention.

"Thank you all for coming." She put a hand on Gran's shoulder. "Now it's time to bring out the birthday cake."

Violet glanced at Chrissy again, gave her a tight

smile, and got up from the table. So far, she was the only person Chrissy had met tonight that hadn't seemed happy to see her there. There were a lot of curious looks, but that was it.

Mrs. Tabor nodded toward the clubhouse, and someone wheeled out the largest birthday cake Chrissy had ever seen. The base itself was as large as a giant pizza box, and it extended upward into three tiers. Roses made of frosting covered the cake, turning it into a mini edible garden. Even this crowd couldn't come close to eating the whole thing. The arrival of the cake was accompanied by appreciative clapping.

Mr. Tabor kissed his mother's cheek. "We opted for one rose-shaped candle on the top."

Gran patted his hand. "That'll be fine, dear. But I'll have you know I was looking forward to the challenge of blowing out ninety candles." She gave him a stern look that quickly dissolved into a playful smile.

Chrissy thoroughly enjoyed watching Gran as she interacted with her family members. When she turned ninety, she hoped she'd continue to live her life with such grace.

Wyatt's hand brushed against Chrissy's shoulder, sending goosebumps traveling down her arm. He leaned in close. "Sorry about my sister. She's naturally the suspicious type. About everything." He was so close to her ear that his breath brushed across her skin like a feather. Chrissy suppressed a sigh as he squeezed her shoulder and let his hand drop.

This whole thing was a charade. So why was his

nearness turning her brain into mush?

~*~

Wyatt really didn't know what he expected from Chrissy at the birthday party. She was good at her job at the coffee shop, and she was well spoken, so he assumed she'd at least be professional about their arrangement. What he hadn't banked on was how easily she inserted herself into his family. By the time Gran had cake and opened the rest of her gifts, Chrissy had visited with all his siblings and even some of the cousins. From what he could tell, she handled each of the conversations with ease.

Not only that, but he could visualize her as a member of his family. That wasn't a good thing.

"Wyatt?"

Gran's voice shook him from his thoughts. He smiled at her, aware of Chrissy to his right. "Hey, Gran. I hope you're having a great party."

"I am, dear, thank you." Gran reached for Chrissy's hand. When she placed it in Wyatt's hand, the warmth of Chrissy's skin practically burned into his. He glanced at her out of the corner of his eye. She covered her surprise and then laced her fingers with his.

That's when Wyatt had to hide his own shock. He gently squeezed her hand and forced his attention back to Gran.

She fingered the necklace that one of her great-grandchildren made her. "It's wonderful to see you with someone, Wyatt. It's about time. And it's been a treat to meet you, Chrissy." She looked thoughtful. "You know, Wyatt, you should bring Chrissy on the family vacation."

Wyatt started to shake his head, but Gran would have none of it. "I insist." She looked at Chrissy imploringly. "Humor an old woman. I'd like to get to know you better, dear. Please do come. Normally, it's our reunion, but I think many of us are already here today." She chuckled. "Ask Wyatt, he can tell you all about it."

"Oh, I don't know…" Chrissy looked lost as she glanced at Wyatt, hoping for a hint on how to respond.

"I'm pretty sure Chrissy has to work that weekend, Gran."

Chrissy nodded.

Gran only looked more serious. "Nonsense. What could be better for a young couple in love than a weekend at the coast? I expect to see you both there." She gently patted Chrissy's cheek and turned to talk to Wyatt's uncle.

Chrissy's hand was still nestled in his as he led her away from Gran and toward the clubhouse. "I guess I should be getting you back home." Wyatt paused once inside and glanced at the watch on his other wrist. "And look at that, it's not quite eight. See, I'm getting you out of here early."

She smiled at him and glanced down at their joined hands. Reluctantly, he released hers and slid both of his into the pockets of his pants. "If you'll follow me, miss, I'll get you through this maze of a country club and escort you home."

Chrissy offered a mock curtsy. "Thank you, kind sir."

Wyatt ridiculously wished he still held her hand as he led the way through the clubhouse and back out to the large circular driveway out front. Once they were seated in his car again, he reached across and withdrew an envelope from the glove compartment. He handed it to Chrissy.

"There you go—the last of the money we agreed on." Unwilling to dawdle in the parking lot and risk someone coming out to talk to them, Wyatt turned the ignition and began to drive them back to her place.

Chrissy slipped the envelope into her purse.

"You don't want to count it?"

"I trust you." She closed her purse again and set it on the floorboard. "Thank you."

"Are you kidding? You saw my family. You went above and beyond tonight. Thank you for being so kind to Gran and for putting up with Violet."

Chrissy laughed then. "Your sister is a character, isn't she? And rightfully suspicious."

"Maybe so, but she doesn't need to know that." He grinned.

Chrissy's smile faded as she kept her gaze fixed on the windshield. She finally cleared her throat. "Look, I wanted you to know that this money is a huge help. It'll go to pay for my own sister's medication this month."

Wyatt glanced at her. She didn't say more, but he detected a catch in her voice. He'd grown up with money—more money than he ever knew what to do with. It sounded stupid and selfish, but sometimes he forgot that so many other people struggled. Wow, now he felt like a snob. The five hundred dollars tonight hadn't even made Wyatt think twice, yet it seemed to mean a lot to Chrissy.

He wished he'd offered to pay her more. "I hope your sister's okay."

"She is now." It didn't sound like Chrissy was going to say more, but then she continued. "Emma had a heart transplant. It saved her life. But the medical bills have been astronomical, and the medication every month alone…" She cleared her throat. "Sorry, none of that is your problem."

Things started falling into place. "So you, your sister, and your mom all live together?"

Chrissy nodded. "By splitting the cost three ways, we can afford to live there. It works out."

"That sounds like a great plan." As Wyatt pulled up in front of her house, he was again struck by how rundown the place was. He wondered if the landlords were just that cheap or if the three women owned the place and couldn't afford to keep it up. A host of questions swirled in his head, but he stopped himself from asking them. He barely knew Chrissy. It wasn't his place to start questioning her financial position or to insert himself into their lives by offering help. It should be enough to know that the money he gave her would purchase medication for her sister.

At least, that's what he kept telling himself as he went around the vehicle, opened the door for Chrissy, and watched as she got out. He saw the curtains in one window part as two people looked out at them.

Chrissy noticed it then, too, and chuckled. "Since they both know about tonight's arrangement, would you like to meet them?"

A flash of panic traveled to his throat, and he swallowed. Would her family want to meet him? What if they were offended by the fact that he paid Chrissy to essentially go on a date with him? "Considering you were willing to talk to my mass of a family, it only seems fair." Wyatt put a hand to her back as they walked up the few stairs to the front door. Spending a little extra time with Chrissy wasn't a bad thing. He hadn't looked forward to saying goodnight and going home quite yet, anyway.

The sounds of the locks turning filtered through the door. Chrissy quickly turned and whispered, "Only stay a few minutes, okay? Emma gets tired in the evening and needs her rest. But don't tell her I said that, or she'll have my head."

Wyatt chuckled. "You've got it."

The door opened, and a woman who looked like a taller and wiser version of Chrissy greeted them. "Oh! I didn't expect... Please, come on in." She smiled brightly and moved to the side.

Wyatt followed Chrissy through the door and

into the small living room where Chrissy's sister waited.

Chrissy wasted no time in introducing everyone. "This is my sister, Emma, and my mom, Sarah. Guys, this is Wyatt."

He shook their hands, relieved to receive what seemed to be a warm welcome from Chrissy's family. "It's wonderful to meet you both. I hope I didn't keep Chrissy out for very long."

"Not at all," Sarah said. "I hope your grandmother is having a wonderful birthday."

"She is, thank you. She thrives on attention, even though she won't admit it." Wyatt laughed. "She loved every minute of having thirty-odd family members there celebrating her birthday." She'd always made a big deal out of everyone else's birthdays, too. Wyatt didn't remember a single birthday of his own without Gran there. In fact, she'd bought him his first remote-controlled car—a toy that he still had even though it had quit working long ago.

Emma motioned toward the little kitchen. "Can I get you something to drink?"

Wyatt held up a hand. "I appreciate it, but no, thank you. I just wanted to say hello before I went home." He discreetly observed the living room and the kitchen where he could just make out the yellow-topped cabinets. Everything inside the house could use an update as well. At the same time, everything was clean and tidy. Clearly, the ladies took great care of what they had, they just didn't seem to have the means to update things as needed.

Sarah motioned to the couch and waited for Wyatt to sit before she joined him. Emma sat in the small recliner, and Chrissy balanced on the arm of the couch near her mother.

"So what do you do for a living, Wyatt?" Sarah asked.

"I manage one of my father's businesses." He shrugged. "It's not overly exciting, but it's a decent job." He didn't want to go into the fact that Dad owned the country club, among other things. Instead of dwelling on whether or not he should tell her, he deflected before more questions could be asked. "What about you, Sarah?"

"I work for Clearwater Community Bank on the other side of town. I have for nearly twenty years now." She smiled. "As you said, it's not overly exciting. But it is a stable job, and one can't complain about that. Especially at my age."

Chrissy reached over and smacked her mother on the arm good-naturedly. "Whatever, Mom."

Sarah only reached up and patted Chrissy's hand.

Wyatt smiled. "It sounds like a great job." He looked at Emma. "How about you?"

"I work for one of the local veterinary hospitals. It's a lot of fun, and I enjoy the opportunity to help animals and their families." She hid a yawn behind one hand.

"Well, it sounds like you've got the most exciting job out of the four of us, hands down." Wyatt glanced at Chrissy and caught the almost nonexistent nod. "I should probably get going. I just wanted to say hello instead of dropping Chrissy off and disappearing." He stood, and the others followed suit.

Sarah looked like she wanted to say more, but she glanced at Emma who was covering another yawn. "Well, it was nice of you to take the time. And no matter the reason, it was good of Chrissy to get out for a change." She gave her daughter a firm look. "She spends way too much time here with us or on her own."

Chrissy dished an identical look right back at her. "And now it's definitely time for you to go." She flashed him a little smile as she opened the front door.

Wyatt waved. "I hope you have a great rest of your evening." He stepped outside and was half surprised when Chrissy followed, closing the door behind her. She walked with him to his Jeep. He stopped and turned to face her. "Your mom and sister seem really nice."

"Yeah, they are. They're both stubborn as the day is long, but they're pretty great."

"And you are the only one in the family without that particular gene?" He raised an eyebrow.

"Exactly." She tried to look serious but failed miserably.

Wyatt grinned when she started chuckling. "You have a great laugh."

Chrissy clasped her hands together behind her back. "Thank you." Her chin dipped a little as though she were trying to hide her face.

"You're welcome. I'd better go. I guess I'll see you at the coffee shop this week?"

"Yeah, I suppose so."

"Good night, Chrissy."

It wasn't easy for Wyatt to get in his car and leave Chrissy behind. There was something about her that made him want to help her. Protect her. Get to know her better. All of which went against every drop of common sense in his body.

By the time he'd driven out of the neighborhood, he'd already decided that he'd be stopping by a certain lady's place of work for a cup of coffee first thing Monday morning.

Chapter Five

When Wyatt walked into Clearwater Coffee on Thursday morning, Chrissy wasn't all that surprised to see him. Honestly, she'd half expected it. While she wouldn't have admitted it to anyone else, she would've been disappointed if he hadn't shown up after seeing him every morning since the birthday party. Unfortunately, between the morning crowd and his hurry to get to his own job, there was little time to talk and discover the reason behind his increase in visits.

Thursday evening, after eating dinner with Mom and Emma, they settled down in the living room to watch an episode or two of their favorite streamed show.

Emma had been dealing with a cold all week. Chrissy glanced at her, concerned about the dark circles under her sister's eyes. Chrissy had already decided that, if Emma didn't feel better in another day or two, she was going to insist on a doctor's visit.

After going to so many doctors over the years, Chrissy understood why Emma was hesitant. But after a heart transplant, Emma really did need to take every precaution.

Chrissy tried not to flinch when Emma sneezed. Instead, she rested her cell phone on the arm of the couch and did her best to focus on the show. When that didn't distract her from worrying about her sister, her mind turned to Wyatt. Just thinking about him coming in every morning with that friendly smile of his made her feel a little better.

She finally picked up her phone and texted him. "You've sure been in a coffee mood this week."

Chrissy really didn't expect him to text back, but maybe a minute or two later, her phone pinged. She switched it to silent when Mom glanced at her, then she pulled the text up to read it.

"I'll be there tomorrow, too."

She wasn't sure what to say to that then smiled as she typed out, "If you do, you should try something besides your usual."

"Why fix what isn't broken?"

It was the winking emoji at the end of his post that made her grin.

Another text came through. "Are you busy Saturday night?"

What?! Chrissy glanced at Mom and Emma who both seemed unaware of her texting conversation with Wyatt. "Why do you ask?"

"LOL Are you or not?"

"I'm never busy on a Saturday night." Or a Friday night, either. Sadly, that was the truth. In fact, what she was doing now was likely to be on repeat through the weekend. Not that it was a bad thing. She enjoyed hanging out with her family. But when she said it out loud— or in text—it sounded lame.

"Then you're free to go to dinner with me."

Chrissy's jaw dropped, and she closed her mouth with a snap before anyone else noticed. What? He wanted to go to dinner? Was he asking her out on a date? Surely not.

She must have taken too long to respond because another text came through.

"I'd like to officially thank you for going to Gran's party. Nothing fancy. Pizza maybe?"

He'd already paid her; he certainly didn't need to take her out to dinner to thank her. But if that was his reason, then this wasn't a date. Which meant agreeing to go would be okay, right? Besides, pizza did sound good.

"Pizza would be great."

"Can I pick you up at six?"

Chrissy ignored the bubbles of excitement in her chest as she typed her response. "Sure."

"Awesome. Have a good evening, okay?"

She stared at the words on her phone and couldn't stop smiling. She was going on a non-date with Wyatt.

~*~

Yes, Wyatt was stopping by Clearwater Coffee for the fifth morning in a row. The caffeine fix certainly helped him face whatever was going on at the country club. But more so, there was something about the smile Chrissy greeted him with that put him in a good mood for the rest of the day. It probably wasn't a good thing that he was starting to get as addicted to that smile as he was to his daily cup of coffee.

He only realized how addicted he was becoming when he walked into the shop and spotted someone else behind the counter in place of Chrissy. He waited in line like he planned. After placing his order, he casually asked, "Is Chrissy working today?"

The woman with a name tag that had "Lil" written on it shook her head. "She was supposed to, but we switched shifts. She called me early, early this morning." Lil put a lid on his cup of coffee and handed it over. "Said she had to get to an unexpected doctor's appointment or something. Anyway, she should be here tomorrow."

Concern balled in his chest as Wyatt accepted the coffee, dropped a tip into the jar, and made his way back out again. Was Chrissy sick? She seemed fine yesterday. What if something was wrong with Emma? He got to the country club and was about to get out of his car when the concern and curiosity got the better of him. He pulled his phone out and sent Chrissy a text. "One of your coworkers said you had to take off today without much notice. I just wanted to make sure everything was okay."

It was silly, but he hoped for an immediate response. He definitely didn't get one. Five minutes later, he sighed and went to work. Chrissy could be in with the doctor right now. Or driving. Or there were any number of other reasons for why she wasn't responding. For that matter, texting back may not be one of her priorities. Their friendship was new, after all.

Did she even count him a friend? Or was he simply one of her frequent coffee customers? Thinking about it made him realize that he did consider her to be a friend. That she felt the same way was more important to him than it ought to be.

When he reached his office at the club, he was surprised to find Violet there waiting for him. She was sitting on the edge of his desk with a hand on one hip as though waiting to scold him about something. Just what he didn't need.

"What's up, Violet?" He walked past her and took a seat in his chair. There was a stack of papers resting on his desk that hadn't been there yesterday evening. Most likely new to-do lists from Dad. He motioned to them. "It looks like I'm going to be busy today." Hopefully Violet would say her piece and go her own way. It wasn't likely, though. Violet took her sweet time about everything, unless it was something *she* thought was important.

"Who was she really?"

"Who was who?"

Violet scowled. "Chrissy. You know, the date you brought to Gran's birthday party? I went by to visit Gran yesterday, and Chrissy was all she could talk about."

"Okay." He was glad Gran liked Chrissy so much, but what did any of this have to do with Violet's visit here? If anything, this was a conversation that might be coming up between him and Gran. He'd deal with that when he had to. Why was Violet so invested in this? "I guess I'm confused as to what any of that has to do with you."

That was probably the wrong phrasing to use. Violet felt anything going on in the family was something she should not only know about, but at least be invited to give her input. She raised an eyebrow and slid off his desk to stand and face him.

"You never mentioned Chrissy before. She doesn't seem your type."

Now it was time for Wyatt to raise an eyebrow at her. "Excuse me? And you know my type?"

Violet only shrugged. "Come on, little brother. You and I both know Chrissy's not the right person to help you get over Ashley. She works at a coffee shop, for goodness' sake. You're nearly thirty-eight. Dad's stressed about making sure the country club stays in the family. And Gran's worried the family name is going to die with you. She's not getting any younger, you know."

"I'm aware of that, thank you. And I don't need

help to get over Ashley—I've been over her for a very long time." His ex was the last person he wanted to talk about. Violet, as well as the rest of his family, knew the kind of hell that woman put him through. He wished he could dismiss her actions as easily as most of them had.

He glared at his oldest sister and wished she'd mind her own business. The last thing he needed was for her to throw Gran into the conversation and try to guilt-trip him into something stupid. One would think that her own marriage and three kids were enough to keep her busy. "And since you don't feel like Chrissy's my type, you think I should be looking elsewhere?"

Violet's eyes narrowed. "She works at a coffee shop, little brother. Her hair..." She trailed off as if what she mentioned alone ought to settle everything. "I can't begin to understand why you asked her to Gran's party. What were you thinking?"

Wyatt stared at her. Violet had certainly shown her true colors many times growing up, but this was a new low. To dismiss Chrissy entirely based on her employment was unacceptable, and he was certain he'd feel that way if Violet was talking about anyone else as well. He stood again, a good six inches taller than his big sister. "You know nothing about Chrissy." He nodded toward the obviously new shoes she was wearing—an obsession of Violet's that she and her husband were in frequent discontent over. "I hardly think you're in a position to judge my girlfriend on how she makes a living." He was surprised to hear the word *girlfriend* leave his lips, but he didn't think Violet noticed.

Instead, he picked up the stack of papers. "If you'll excuse me, I've got some work to do." He heard her huff and puff as she left the room and closed his office door harder than necessary behind her. Only then did Wyatt sink into his desk chair again with a groan.

Violet was like a bulldog who didn't let anything go until she'd shaken the life out of it. He'd like to think she would go on her merry way and leave Chrissy out of everything, but he knew better than that.

His thoughts settled on Chrissy. Sure, she was different from any other woman he dated. And Violet was right about one thing: Chrissy didn't fit what would've been considered his type. But seeing how things had ended in the past, maybe that wasn't such a bad thing.

Wyatt checked his phone and wished she'd text him back. Just because she'd agreed to go out with him Saturday night did not mean they were in a relationship. If they were, he'd know what was going on. And Wyatt certainly didn't need Violet to remind him of how disastrous his last relationship was. Every detail was etched into his brain as well as his self-confidence. He resisted the temptation to text Chrissy a second time and tried to focus on his work.

~*~

Chrissy placed a cup of hot peppermint tea on the table next to the couch where Emma was resting. Her head was on a pillow with one arm curled beneath it. She gave Chrissy a small, tired smile. "Thanks, sis."

"You're welcome." She sat down on the worn recliner nearby. Everything about the day had been exhausting, from the moment she'd awakened at three in the morning to sounds of Emma coughing and wheezing until she'd returned with medication from the pharmacy not long ago at two in the afternoon. She stifled a yawn.

"You should go take a nap," Emma said, her words punctuated with a round of coughing.

Chrissy shook her head. "I'm good here." She crossed her arms for emphasis and leaned into the recliner, a spot in the back poking into her ribs like it always did. One of those comforting annoyances.

The sounds of Mom working in the kitchen filtered into the living room. She was making chicken soup despite Emma insisting she wasn't hungry. Chrissy completely understood the need to feel busy. That's why there was a cup of tea sitting nearby completely untouched.

Emma's eyes drifted closed. Chrissy stared at her sister. Bronchitis was nothing to play around with anyway, but when Emma's immune system was as compromised as it was, this could be dangerous. She'd spent a good part of the day receiving fluids and breathing treatments. They had a whole list of things to watch for. If Emma developed a high fever, or if the breathing treatments they could now do at home didn't help, they were to take her to the emergency room.

Emma didn't want to talk about the fact that her job was making her sick more often than normal, but it was something she was going to have to address sooner rather than later. Working at the desk instead of directly with the animals helped, but she was still around all the hair and dander. And even if Emma wouldn't admit it, Chrissy was certain she was still helping with the animals at times. It'd be nearly impossible not to in that situation, especially when Emma loved them so much.

Needless to say, Chrissy would be taking shifts with Mom to be certain Emma was doing okay and that her health wasn't deteriorating through the night.

Chrissy yawned, and this time she didn't try to keep it hidden. She pulled her phone out and read Wyatt's text for the sixth time that day. She'd kept meaning to text him back, but then something vied for her attention again.

"I can't tell if you're avoiding someone or stalking him." Emma's voice made Chrissy jump, which only elicited a smile. "Seriously, you should just call him."

"I have no idea what you're talking about." Chrissy turned her screen off and put the phone under her leg. "Speaking of avoiding something…"

Emma immediately shook her head. "I don't want to talk about that right now." Another round of coughing plus Mom coming in with a steaming bowl of soup effectively ended the conversation.

Mom got Emma set up with her soup and turned on a television program. Now that Mom was there, Chrissy excused herself. Instead of going to the kitchen, she stepped out onto the tiny back porch. There was just enough room for a pair of folding lawn chairs that had certainly seen better days. Chrissy eased herself into one, amazed as always that the plastic bands didn't just snap and send her to the ground.

She opened her texts and started to respond to Wyatt. She'd gotten a sentence or two in when she changed her mind. She erased everything and, before she lost her nerve, called him instead.

"Hello?"

Just the sound of his deep voice set butterflies loose in her stomach. "Hey. It's Chrissy. Sorry I didn't text sooner."

"It's okay. I figured something must be going on. Are you all right?"

"We had to take Emma to the emergency room just after three this morning. We only got back home a little while ago." She stretched her legs out and allowed the back of her head to rest against the top of the chair.

"Oh, wow. I'm sorry to hear that." There was some background sound, like shuffling papers, that came through the phone. "Is she okay?"

Chrissy realized that it was only four o'clock. Wyatt was probably still at work. "She has bronchitis. Obviously that's no fun for anyone, but the medications she takes to keep her body from rejecting her heart also lowers her immune system. It doesn't take much for her to go from bronchitis to pneumonia. We're going to have to watch her closely for a few days." She paused. "I just realized you're probably working. I didn't think of that. I should've just texted."

"Are you kidding? You've been on my mind all day. Since I've never seen you miss a day of work before, I figured something major must have happened."

He'd been thinking about her? Chrissy had been so concerned about Emma all day that the idea of being the focus of someone else's worry sent tendrils of warmth through her. She pictured his kind, green eyes and couldn't keep a smile from lifting the corners of her mouth. She'd missed seeing him this morning. "You're right. I'm somewhat of a workaholic. Although I'll be working tomorrow now to make up for it." She wasn't keen on the idea. At least Mom would be home with Emma all day. She'd call if Emma started feeling worse.

"You'll get a lunch break, I assume."

"I will. Usually at one." Most of the time, Chrissy spent her lunch breaks in a corner booth at the coffee shop eating a sandwich and browsing social media on her phone. She couldn't help but hope Wyatt was asking about her schedule for a reason.

"How about I stop by and we take a walk or something?"

Chrissy grinned, fully aware that her family would be making fun of her right now if they saw. "I'd like that."

"Great." He paused. "If there's anything I can do to help, please let me know. I hope your sister feels better soon."

"Thank you." She wasn't ready to hang up yet but knew he needed to get back to work. Besides, what else was she going to talk about? "I guess I should let you go. I'll see you tomorrow."

"See you then. Get some rest, Chrissy."

His thoughtfulness settled over her heart like a warm blanket.

Chapter Six

"On second thought, maybe my suggestion of going for a walk wasn't the best idea." Wyatt frowned at the cloudless sky. The relentless summer heat they'd been experiencing all week hadn't eased now that it was the weekend. If anything, the humidity had increased.

Chrissy moved to stand in the shade of a large tree. "It amazes me every time I sell a cup of hot coffee during the summer." She raised an eyebrow. "And yes, that includes you, too."

Wyatt shifted to stand next to her and welcomed the break from the sun. "So you only drink iced coffee during the summer?"

"I don't drink coffee at all. I can't stand the taste."

He watched her face, expecting her to say she was joking, but her expression remained deadpan. "You work at a coffee shop, and you don't drink coffee."

"I'm pretty sure that if I did like coffee, I wouldn't after smelling it for hours on end." She chuckled. "Don't worry. I work for the scones."

"Well, I'm glad there's some incentive." Wyatt watched as she reached for a leaf on the tree and pulled it off before fiddling with it in her hand. The movement brought his attention to her wrist and the tattoo there. Before he realized what he was doing, he'd reached out and touched one of the heart-shaped rosebuds with the tip of a finger. "Your tattoo is one of the most detailed I've seen, especially for one so delicate. Is there meaning behind it?"

Chrissy dropped the leaf and rubbed her opposite thumb over the vine on her wrist with a shrug. "You know how people plant a tree for loved ones they've lost? I guess this is my version of that."

Wyatt counted three flowers incorporated into the tattoo, suddenly aware of what they meant. "I think that's a thoughtful way of remembering them." He wanted to ask what each one stood for but wasn't sure if she'd welcome the intrusion into her life.

She seemed to consider her options before clearing her throat. She touched a pale red bud. "This one is for my dad. He died in a construction accident just after Emma was born. Mom has told me all about him many times, but I wish I had more of my own memories." Her fingertip moved to brush against the purple bud. "My grandma died when I was twelve, but she had a profound effect on my life. I still hear her voice inside my head, encouraging me to do my best."

Chrissy chuckled. "I have a strong inkling that she and your gran would get along wonderfully."

The thought of that made Wyatt smile in return. At the same time, he was saddened by the realization that she was missing out on the relationship he treasured with Gran. Why was it so easy to take for granted what he had in his life? "And this one?" He touched the fully bloomed yellow rose and tried to ignore the electrical charge that traveled from the point of connection straight to his heart, giving it a jolt.

"That's to remind me that death isn't forever. That even though I'm missing my family here on Earth, I know I'll see them again someday. And that gives me hope." She gave a little shrug. "It probably sounds really lame, but knowing God's there and more in control of things than I am is what got me through Emma's condition and transplant."

"I don't think that sounds lame at all. I think it's a beautiful reminder." Memories of holding her hand at Gran's birthday party flooded his mind, and he resisted the urge to reach for it now. He had a thought and jerked a thumb toward the street. "Do you like snow cones?"

That brought a smile to Chrissy's face and seemed to chase away the mixed emotions that were there before. "Absolutely." She pointed at him. "As long as you promise to not make fun of my flavor choice."

He held up both hands, palms out in surrender. "I wouldn't dare." Now she had him curious. "Shall we?"

They walked side by side down the street to the little shack five minutes away. They served two things: hot dogs and snow cones. There were two round tables complete with umbrellas to block the sun's heat. They only had to wait for one customer before it was their turn to order.

Wyatt motioned for Chrissy to order first. She tossed him a look that reminded him of his promise, then she turned and ordered a bubble gum snow cone. He wasn't sure if he thought it was cute, quirky, or both.

When he ordered orange, she scoffed at him. They both also ordered a hot dog. Only after the person who took their orders went to make the snow cones did she chuckle. "Here I thought you'd be the type to get adventurous and order the red velvet cake or the s'mores flavor."

He raised an eyebrow at her. "You first, and I'll think about it."

Chrissy reached for the pink snow cone and cupped it in both hands. "I'm good, thanks." She tossed him a saucy look and moved to sit at one of the tables. A moment later, Wyatt joined her. Even if the ambient air was still humid and hot, the shade from the umbrella was a welcome change. He relaxed into the back of his metal chair and scooped up a spoonful of his snow cone. The moment the ice crystals melted in his mouth, he knew this was the right choice. "You know," he began, pointing to his treat, "I may have to switch up my routine and come here every morning instead. I wonder if they have a coffee flavor…" He twisted in his seat and pretended to look over the menu behind him. When he turned back, she was looking at him, her eyes sparkling.

"And you thought bubble gum was weird." She laughed.

Wyatt wasn't a fan of bubble gum, though he had a feeling he'd like it a lot better if he tasted it on her lips. His wayward thoughts surprised him, and he fought against the temptation to see if he was right. He jabbed a spoon into his snow cone a little more forcefully than necessary. The last time he'd let himself get close to a woman was Ashley, and she'd stabbed him in the back. He'd sworn he would never put himself in that position again. Yet, here he was. The connection he felt with Chrissy was more than just a passing interest. Not that he ought to do anything about it. He tried to ignore the disappointment that flooded his system and fought desperately for a change in subject.

"How's your sister doing?" He regretted the question the moment Chrissy's smile dipped.

"She should be resting today. The doctor told her she couldn't go back to work until Monday." She paused. "Truthfully, she needs to quit her job at the vet hospital."

"Why's that?" Wyatt ate another spoonful of snow cone and then drank some of the syrup through a straw since it was melting at a fast rate.

"After her transplant, the doctor warned her that working with the animals was putting her at risk. There are just too many germs and hair, which increases her chance of getting sick. The doctor thinks that's what aggravated her lungs and turned allergy symptoms into bronchitis." She stirred her snow cone with the spoon but then left it in the bright pink mixture. "Instead of leaving her job as a vet tech, her boss lets her work up front most of the time. It minimizes her contact with the animals. I don't think it's enough, though." Chrissy's shoulders slumped. "Emma needs something to focus on, and she loves that job. But her health is more important. At the same time, I'm not sure how we're going to keep on financially if she doesn't find another job."

Wyatt could almost see the concrete weights that were pushing her shoulders down. He'd never had to worry about finances—both a blessing and a curse—but he could certainly imagine the pressures and worries he'd experience if one of his sisters were in such a fragile medical state. "I'm sorry things are so complicated."

"Me, too." She released a long sigh and glanced at him. She visibly tried to push her thoughts behind her and sat up straighter. "Enough about that. So tell me about this family vacation your Gran invited me to."

Wyatt rolled his eyes. "It's three days of more food than anyone could possibly eat, laughter, annoyances, and embarrassments. You know, everything you'd expect from a large family reunion."

"And you go every year."

"Of course." He grinned, suddenly wishing that he could ask Chrissy to go with him. If he did, it would only make things worse with his family when it came to their relationship. Or lack thereof. He loved his family, but there was a certain sister that could make Chrissy's life miserable, and he didn't want to subject Chrissy to that. Besides, what was it going to accomplish? He'd promised himself he wouldn't be put in a position like he was with Ashley.

Chrissy seemed to take everything in as he shared about some of the family antics. He couldn't help but drink in the sound of her laughter and bask in her smiles. He may not want to let himself care about Chrissy, but he already felt more for her than he should. If he were an intelligent man, he'd put some space between them.

"Are your sisters looking forward to the reunion?"

Her voice reminded Wyatt to simply focus on the conversation. He shrugged. "It depends on who you're talking about. Lucy loves everything about it. She's super sentimental and is the one who's taking pictures of everyone and everything. I think it's her favorite event of the year."

"And she's the second oldest, right?"

"Good memory. Now Violet likes it for an entirely different reason." He never knew where the line was between gossiping about his sister and giving people fair warning. "Violet likes to play people against each other. I know that's horrible to say of my own sister, but it's true. Thankfully, nearly everyone knows that. But she still manages to stir some pots year after year." A small, welcome breeze came through and swept some of his hair into his eyes. He brushed it away. "I think Bonnie is more like I am. We go because we should. We enjoy seeing family that we don't see otherwise, but we're really not the big group types."

Wyatt drank the last of his melted snow cone, the straw making a slurping sound at the end. "That was good, though I think it melted in record time."

Chrissy tipped her paper cup to show him the pink liquid at the bottom. "No kidding." She plopped her spoon into it. Only then did she turn her focus to her hot dog. Wyatt had devoured his minutes ago. "This place was a great idea. Thank you."

"You're welcome." Here was the part where he could easily dismiss their agreement to eat dinner tonight. He was sure she was worried about Emma, and he probably did need to put some space between them. Then again, he never was great about listening to his own advice. "I do want to take you out somewhere that has more than two tables." They laughed. "Are we still on for pizza tonight?" He would certainly understand if she felt like she needed to stay home with Emma. The selfish part of him, however, hoped that she'd say yes.

She looked uncertain as she glanced at her phone, probably checking for texts. "I'm not sure."

When she realized he was watching her, she sat up straighter. "I should probably see how Emma's doing when I get back from work first, and I don't want you to have to wait until the last minute. Maybe it would be better if we cancel tonight?"

Chrissy was probably right, but just the thought disappointed Wyatt. "I completely understand, but I promise last minute doesn't bother me. Why don't you check on Emma and then text me either way?"

"Are you sure?"

Even as she asked the question, she seemed to relax a little. Was it possible she was looking forward to dinner tonight as much as he was? That thought bolstered Wyatt's confidence. "I'm sure. And if you feel like you need to stay with Emma, maybe we can reschedule for the next evening or two."

"That sounds great. Thank you."

The way her happy smile made Wyatt's heart turn over both amazed and scared him. How could this beautiful woman have gotten under his skin so quickly? The panic he felt at the realization still didn't overpower how much he was looking forward to their date. Seriously, it was one date. It wasn't like he was going to ask her to marry him or something. He'd learned his lesson last time.

So he'd take Chrissy out for pizza, enjoy the conversation, and not worry about the future. Surely there was nothing wrong with that.

Chapter Seven

"Uh oh. What happened?" There was no missing the dark expression on Emma's face the moment Chrissy walked into the house. Instead of responding, Emma held up her inhaler and continued with her breathing treatment. Chrissy patted her knee. "All right. I'm going to go shower and get this coffee smell off me. I'll be back."

Emma nodded as she breathed in the steam. The image of her in pajamas with the breathing treatment didn't exactly make Chrissy feel confident about leaving again later in the evening. By the time she finished showering, she'd already decided to text and cancel dinner with Wyatt. She just hadn't actually done it yet.

With her phone in hand, she wandered back to the living room where Emma had finished her breathing treatment and was perusing the channels on TV—all five of them—with a frown on her face.

"You look like they just canceled your favorite show." Chrissy plopped herself down on the couch. "Where's Mom?"

"She ran down to the store. She said she'd be back in twenty minutes."

They'd already been through the list of channels three times when Chrissy took the remote and set it on the coffee table. "I could've stopped on my way back from work."

Emma didn't respond. Instead, she watched the laundry detergent commercial on TV with the attention of her favorite movie.

Chrissy sighed and turned the TV off entirely. "You're starting to freak me out. Did the doctor call you or something?" Organ rejection was constantly in the back of Chrissy's mind. What if the doctor had gotten some tests back and found evidence that things weren't going as smoothly as they thought? What if this was more than just bronchitis? All those old worries about losing her sister flooded Chrissy.

Emma looked at her and must've seen the emotion in her eyes because she put an arm around Chrissy and pulled her close. "No, it's nothing like that. I'm sorry, I forget that's the first place you and Mom go to." She let her head rest against Chrissy's. "My boss called and asked me to quit my job. He's paying me for all of my vacation days, plus another week." She paused. "He said he feels like it's a liability for me to work there, and he's worried about my health."

"He's not wrong."

"Yeah, I know." Emma moved her arm to cover a cough and slouched against the back of the couch. "I need to find another job now. How many places are going to hire someone who gets sick all the time?"

"Well, for one thing, hopefully you won't be getting sick all the time now that you're not working at the vet's office." Chrissy cringed when Emma flinched. "I'm sorry. Seriously, I know how much you loved that job. It's what you always wanted to do, and after all you've been through, it's not fair that you have to give that up." Memories of Emma taking care of the neighborhood pets and bringing home stray after stray came to mind. Emma never had a plan B because becoming a vet tech was always the goal.

Truthfully, Chrissy had envied Emma and her drive. It would've been nice to have a goal like that to shoot for. She never thought she'd be working at a coffee shop long-term.

The reality of a third of their combined income disappearing hit Chrissy hard. Hopefully Emma would get another job, but she was sick now and needed to take time to rest. Realistically, Chrissy should probably look for a second job. Different options raced through her mind until Emma elbowed her.

"I thought you had a hot date tonight."

Wyatt. Right, she should probably text him and cancel before it got much later. Chrissy ignored the flash of disappointment. "Are you kidding? I thought we'd hang out and watch one of your favorite movies."

Emma pinned her down with a knowing look.

"We do that nearly every night. You can't keep putting your life on hold because of me. Go on your date and get out for a while."

"I second that." Mom's voice snagged their attention as she pushed the front door open the rest of the way and stepped inside. "I'm making a casserole tonight. If it were me, I'd be going somewhere else for dinner." She winked. "We've got this."

Chrissy wanted to protest, but with the two of them looking at her, she knew she wasn't going to win. Besides, she did want to see Wyatt again. When she was around him, she was somehow able to forget many of the worries that plagued her daily. It was freeing, in a way, even as some guilt pummeled her for feeling that way at all.

She finally caved under their matching scrutiny. "Fine. I'll go. But you have to promise me you'll call if anything comes up and I need to come home. Okay?"

Only after she'd gotten a verbal promise from them both did Chrissy text Wyatt and let him know that she was still good for pizza. Frankly, even though her mom was a great cook, Chrissy never was a fan of her casseroles.

~*~

Chrissy took a bite of pizza and relished the double cheese melted over pepperoni and black olives. Oh, man, she'd missed this. She didn't realize how much she was focused on her pizza until Wyatt's chuckles grounded her. "Sorry. I haven't had pizza in way too long."

"Really?" He looked surprised. "I try to eat it every Friday night. Maybe it's not the healthiest meal, but it's worth it. If you don't like pizza, we could've gone somewhere else."

"It's not a matter of not liking it. It's Emma...She's got a pretty restrictive diet now, and pizza used to be one of her favorite foods. So Mom and I make a point of not eating it around her, either." She shrugged. "It's worth it to keep her healthy."

His mood seemed to sober a little. "You and your mom do a lot for Emma."

She might have taken offense at his words, except there was admiration in his voice.

"We do a lot for each other. It's just the three of us, really. There was a time we thought we were going to lose Emma. It's nothing short of a miracle that she's still with us now." She paused. "God spared her life. Not eating pizza seems like such an incredibly small price to pay."

"I'm glad she's doing a little better tonight." He paused. "I admit to knowing little about transplants and what happens afterward. Will she be on this medication long term?"

"She's taking seven medications now, and most will be for the rest of her life. They just may be adjusted a little over time as Emma's needs change." Chrissy took another bite of her pizza and chewed thoughtfully. "She found out today that she lost her job at the vet's office."

Wyatt frowned with concern. "I'm sorry to hear that. Although it sounds like you weren't surprised."

"I'm not. And honestly, Emma will probably be healthier by no longer working there. But she's stressed about not contributing to the household income. And her meds…" Chrissy shrugged. "We'll figure everything out. Just when we think we've reached our limits, God has something planned to remind us we're not completely on our own. But it is a little overwhelming in the meanwhile."

The worried look on Wyatt's face was sweet. At the same time, the last thing Chrissy wanted was for him to feel sorry for her family. This was a rough situation; there was no doubt about it. But if they could get through waiting to see if Emma would get a transplant and wondering whether her body would reject the heart, they could make it through this.

He'd set down his piece of sausage pizza and was watching her thoughtfully. It was time she changed the subject.

"So, I've realized I'm a horrible conversationalist."

That got his attention. He raised an amused eyebrow at her. "Oh? What makes you say that?"

"Because we've talked about your family, the reunion, and yet I've failed to ask you what it is you do for work. Obviously, you either drive by the coffee shop or work in the area." She used a napkin to wipe the grease from her fingers. "You mentioned that you manage a place for your father. What business is it?"

She hadn't expected the hesitation and momentary flash of uncertainty in his eyes. Chrissy chuckled. "What? Is your father a mortician? Because I do find that a little creepy, though I guess someone has to do it, right?"

She'd hoped her teasing might make him feel more at ease, but his expression hadn't changed. What was it, then? Was his family part of the mob? Surely not. She hadn't spoken to his parents much at the birthday party, but they seemed pretty normal. What was he so reluctant to tell her? Uncertainty hit her as she realized how little she knew about him. For every fact she'd learned over the last week or two, there had to be a hundred more that she had no clue about. Of course, the same was true for him and how little he knew about her as well. "Sorry, I thought it was just a normal question. You don't have to tell me."

"No, you're right. It is a normal question." He ran a hand through his hair. "I do manage my father's business." He paused. "My family owns the country club, among other things."

Chrissy let that news sink in. She remembered reading an article in the newspaper about the country club and how the man who owned it was a multi-millionaire. Did that mean Wyatt was just as wealthy? Why hadn't she paid attention to the names back then? She racked her brain trying to remember if there were details of the other businesses the Tabors owned and ran.

"Your family owns the fancy country club where your grandmother's party was held? That's what you manage?" She'd thought it was a strange place for a birthday party. But to celebrate ninety years, she figured they'd gone all out by renting the clubhouse. She'd had no idea... Wow.

No wonder he didn't hesitate to pay her to go to Gran's birthday party. His family probably dished that out for toilet paper at some fancy grocery store. And here she'd been talking about her financial woes. Her cheeks heated with embarrassment.

Things may be difficult, but she, Mom, and Emma had it under control. They'd been handling things on their own for a long time, and they didn't need charity.

Wait, what if he thought she already knew and talking about their financial issues was a ploy to get money out of him? She used her fingers to rub her temples. "I had no idea. When I was talking about my sister's medication, I promise I wasn't trying to—"

Wyatt stopped her mid-sentence. "I never thought you were." He reached across the table and squeezed one of her hands. "I find people tend to judge me based on my family alone. I'd prefer people get to know me first before they make a connection between my father and me."

All Chrissy could think about was the way he was watching her so closely and the feel of her hand in his. It was crazy how such a simple gesture had her scrambling to put together one complete thought.

Honestly, she couldn't blame him for not throwing the details of his family's money into the first conversation he had with everyone. It'd be easy for people to make assumptions. While their situations were very different, Chrissy certainly understood why he didn't want to be judged based on his social status. The fact that Wyatt didn't seem to throw money around to get what he wanted said a lot about him.

She cleared her throat. He was still watching her, waiting for a response. Her gaze rested on their joined hands a moment before she shifted her attention to his face. "I get it. It's easy for people to hear one or two things about someone else and think they know everything about them." He visibly relaxed, and Chrissy had to make herself remove her hand from his and continue eating her meal. She instantly missed the connection. "That's neat that you're able to keep the country club in the family like that. I imagine it can be an interesting place to work."

"It has its moments." He took a sip of his soft drink. "Honestly, it's a big juggling act. Keeping customers happy, hiring the right people. There are a lot more politics involved than I care for. I'd much rather stay in the background and work behind the scenes."

Chrissy hadn't paid that much attention when she'd gone there for the party. She knew very little about the place. "So what kind of amenities are offered?"

"Everything from a large golf course and tennis

courts to a day spa. And you saw the clubhouse." Wyatt shrugged. "We've added to the place several times over the last ten years."

"That's great." She smiled at him, unsure of what to say next. She tried to picture herself going to the country club with her mom and sister and couldn't quite do it.

Wyatt must have sensed her train of thought. "It's okay if it's not something you're interested in. It's not really my scene, either. But it's a good job, and trust me, my dad doesn't let my work slide."

"Do your sisters work there as well?"

"No, I'm the only one who runs it with my dad. For better or worse." He laughed. "How about you? What brought you to the coffee shop?"

Chrissy willed herself not to blush. Again. Compared to his job at the country club, managing a coffee shop and making beverages for other people seemed pretty lame. "It's a stable job that has always been able to accommodate my needs for random days off to help Emma." She shrugged. "Now that she's more stable, I've considered a change in employment. Or possibly a second job. But, unlike my sister, I never really went to college. I like where I work and the people I work with, so I'm content for now while I look at my options."

"There's nothing wrong with working there. Having a job that's stable and fits your needs is worth a great deal. I went to college, but I firmly believe that it's not for everyone. It doesn't make what you do any less important." He flashed her a grin that had her heart working overtime. "Goodness knows you feed my coffee addiction. Not to mention seeing that smile of yours always starts my day off on the right foot."

She ducked her head, unable to keep the heat from her face. He had no idea how his presence every morning helped her, too. Instead of dreading her job or feeling as though the coffee shop were some form of the movie Groundhog Day, she woke up every morning and looked forward to seeing him again.

Was that pathetic? She wasn't even sure.

Chrissy had to remind herself that this wasn't a date. Wyatt had stressed that this was supposed to be a meal to thank her for going to Gran's birthday party. Just because he'd been by the coffee shop every day this last week didn't mean he'd continue to do so. In fact, if it weren't for seeing him there, she'd likely never run into him again. They were in very different places in their lives.

She'd enjoy visiting with him tonight and then move forward.

Chrissy struggled to ignore the sadness that seeped into her heart.

Chapter Eight

Wyatt listened as Pastor Donovan said the final prayer of Sunday morning and wished everyone a wonderful week. Wyatt spent several moments shaking the hands of people he'd known most of his life. He'd been coming here with Gran, Bonnie, and Lucy since he was young. It wasn't that their parents didn't believe in God, they just didn't talk about Him much. Church certainly wasn't on their list of priorities.

That's when Gran stepped in. She took the siblings to church, taught them about the ways God touched their every day lives, and was the example of faith and consistency they needed. Violet used to go as well, but eventually chose to walk away from it.

Sundays were still one of Wyatt's favorite days of the week. He got to see Bonnie, Lucy and her family, and his grandmother. He and Gran usually went out to lunch together afterward.

Speaking of Gran, he found her near the front of

the church visiting with one of her friends. As soon as she saw him, she smiled and excused herself. "There you are. I don't know about you, but I'm starving."

"Me, too. Where are we going this week?"

Half an hour later, they were seated at a little café working on their soup and sandwiches. This was the place Gran preferred most weeks, though occasionally she surprised him. Wyatt didn't mind, as this place made the best French dip sandwiches.

"So what does this coming week look like for you, Gran?"

She dabbed at her mouth with a napkin and then laid it across her lap. "Well, that all depends on you."

Wyatt blinked, completely taken by surprise. "I'm not sure what you mean."

Gran made a "tsk-tsk" sound and shook her head sadly. "I spoke with your mother, and it would seem there's no room reservation for Chrissy at the resort. I thought for sure you would invite her. We'd all love the opportunity to get to know her better." She sat up a little straighter. "Unless she's sharing your room. You know how I feel about that, young man. But if it means she'll be joining us, I suppose I can turn a blind eye."

Heat climbed the back of his neck, and Wyatt held up a hand to stop her. "No, we aren't staying in the same room, Gran. I'm pretty sure she has plans with her mom and sister this weekend."

"Surely she could make an exception."

Wyatt studied Gran, but there was no playful glint in her eye like he'd expected. How could he explain that Chrissy wasn't really his girlfriend? Sure, they'd gone out on one date, but that had ended awkwardly. He wasn't sure what had shifted during the close of dinner, and he didn't know where they stood now. There was no way he was going into all of that with Gran, though.

"I just don't think it's going to work out this time, Gran."

Gran sighed, and her shoulders sagged a little. "I understand, Wyatt. I was really hoping she could be there. You know, when I blew out my candle at my birthday party, that was my one wish—that we would see you and Chrissy attend the reunion together."

Wyatt knew very well that Gran was being dramatic, yet he still felt guilty for not bringing his nonexistent girlfriend with him. Wow, Gran was good. What was he supposed to say? There was no way he could ask Chrissy to go with him, especially not after Violet's less-than-subtle attempts to stick her nose into everything. "I'd bring her if I could." He got up and pressed a kiss to her cheek. "I'm sorry to disappoint you."

"That's okay, Wyatt." She patted him on the shoulder. "As my only grandson, you've always made me proud. I know that, if you can at all, you'll find a way to convince that girl of yours to join us. I haven't given up hope yet." Gran gave him a sweet smile. "So what do you have going on this coming week?"

Wyatt sat down again and told her about the work waiting for him at the country club. With several new people to hire, he'd had a lot of applications and resumes to go through.

Gran ate the last spoonful of soup and observed him with a serious look on her face. "Don't work too hard, Wyatt. It's not good for anyone." She paused. "I've watched your father work his life away. I want better for you."

Wyatt recalled many times where Dad hadn't been present due to one work commitment or another. Wyatt grew up determined not to be that way if he ever had a family of his own. "Don't worry, Gran. I know there are a lot of things that are more important than work and making money."

"Good." Gran seemed happy with his answer. "I'm serious about Chrissy, though. It's not every day you meet a girl as sweet as she is. Do what you can to convince her to come to the reunion."

"I can't promise anything."

She seemed content with his answer and went on to talk about the next church social. He admired her ability to speak her mind and not worry what anyone else thought. Gran once told him it was a perk when she reached her eighties, and she'd certainly taken full advantage of it over the years.

Gran had a habit of making things a bigger deal than they needed to be, but that whole bit about wishing for Chrissy to join them for the reunion only echoed his own thoughts. It didn't help that the idea of spending an entire weekend with Chrissy wasn't exactly the worst one he'd ever heard.

~*~

Chrissy slid a finger beneath the flap of the elegant envelope and gently opened it. The only mail she ever got was either bills or junk. This paper looked like something someone would choose for a fancy wedding invitation. That, in combination with the first-class stamp in the upper right corner, told her this was something more.

Curious, she slid a card out, only then aware of Emma watching over her shoulder. Chrissy didn't realize it until it was too late to keep Emma from reading the note as well.

My Dear Chrissy,

It was so kind of you to accompany Wyatt to my birthday party. Thank you for the chocolate truffles. They were delicious. I think, however, the best gift of all was the opportunity to meet the girl that has turned my grandson's head.

I'm still holding out hope that you'll be joining us for the family reunion. Consider it this old woman's true birthday wish. I'd love the opportunity to get to know you better.

Have a delightful week,

Gran

Emma's mouth transformed into a big grin as she turned her head to look at Chrissy. "You turned his head, huh? Why didn't I hear about this?"

"Because Gran's impression of things was a lot different than mine." Chrissy folded the card and put it back into the envelope again. Next time she got a piece of fancy correspondence, she'd be sure she was alone when she read it.

"I love that you're calling her 'Gran' as though it's nothing." Emma put a hand on her hip and raised an eyebrow.

"Everyone there called her Gran. I have no doubt the mailman calls her that, too. I couldn't hurt her feelings—it was her birthday." Chrissy tossed her sister a look of annoyance. "You're making this into way more than it ought to be."

"Then the date last night didn't go well? I was hoping you'd volunteer some information without me having to ask first, but…" Emma's voice trailed off as she feigned a look of disappointment.

Chrissy might have given her a good-natured shove except that she was still worried about Emma's health. Instead, she turned and headed to her bedroom, eager to put the note in her dresser drawer. If she was lucky at all, Emma would forget all about it.

Instead, Emma followed her. "It was that bad, huh?"

Chrissy groaned and allowed herself to fall backward onto her bed. She stared at the ceiling. "No, it wasn't that bad. It was just… Well, I found out his family owns the country club along with a dozen other businesses, and they probably have a finger in just about everything that goes on in town."

Emma's eyes widened appropriately. She eased herself onto the bed beside her sister. "Wow. I didn't see that one coming."

"At least I'm not the only one." She shrugged. "You know why I went to that birthday party. While we were there, Wyatt's grandmother invited me to join them at a family vacation. Or reunion. Something like that. Anyway, it's this weekend. Apparently I played the role of his date too convincingly."

"Oh, really?" Emma turned her head and waggled her eyebrows suggestively. "Just what did you do to convince Gran that you two were really a couple?"

Chrissy closed her eyes and tried to push the memory of holding hands from her mind. Instead, it only intensified. "He held my hand. Once. Seriously, that was it."

"You two must have some major chemistry."

"Emma." Chrissy's note of warning went unnoticed.

"Come on, let me live vicariously through you." Emma turned on her side and propped her head up on her hand. "So you like Wyatt, or at least I'm assuming you do or you wouldn't have gone out with him last night. And there's at least enough chemistry between the two of you to convince his family that you were really together at the party. What would be so bad about going to the family reunion? Let's face it, you could use a vacation."

Chrissy copied her sister's movements and was soon staring at her. "And leave you and Mom? Not a chance."

"You're my sister, Chrissy, not my nurse. You need to live a little. Do something for you. Mom would agree with me, you know."

That was true, but it didn't mean she should traipse off halfway across Texas and leave them behind. If something happened to Emma while she was gone, Chrissy would never forgive herself. Besides, there was no way she was going to crash Wyatt's family reunion. How crazy would that be?

She sighed. "You're not wrong. But it's so much easier said than done." How many times had she and Emma daydreamed together about traveling the world? They'd planned on going to Hawaii, Australia, and Ireland. Maybe even Paris one day. And here they'd never even been out of Texas. How sad was that? She let herself roll onto her back again.

Emma joined her and reached over to lay a hand on Chrissy's shoulder. "I know, sis. I know." She remained silent for a moment.

Why did things like this have to be so hard? "What about you? Any thoughts on your job situation?"

Emma slowly shook her head. "Nah. I don't suppose Wyatt has a brother. Is marrying someone with a lot of money a valid employment option?" She looked at Chrissy, her face serious, and then burst out in laughter.

It wasn't long before Chrissy was laughing so hard she couldn't catch her breath. Marrying a millionaire would certainly solve their money issues, but she had a feeling anything with Wyatt would be more complicated than she could possibly prepare for.

Chapter Nine

Wyatt watched Bonnie as she finished hitting the last three baseballs that were launched her way. When the pitching machine powered down, she lowered her bat and turned with a satisfied look on her face. "We need to do this more often."

He wasn't going to argue with her. In fact, he hadn't felt this relaxed in months. They'd just finished their second round at the country club batting cages. Wyatt's biceps were already aching. Bonnie was right, it'd been way too long since they'd last done this. It used to be a monthly event for them. In fact, they used to call it their gripe session. When everything about their family would drive them crazy, they'd both save up their grievances, go to the batting cage to take it out on the baseballs, and then talk.

They dropped their gear off, grabbed cold

bottles of water, and found a small table in a more secluded area of the gardens. Wyatt downed half his water in several swallows before securing the top again and leaning back in his chair. "You were hitting those balls pretty hard. Whose face were you picturing?"

Bonnie giggled. She'd always had a little girl laugh that was highly contagious, and Wyatt had yet to meet someone who was impervious to it. She took another sip of water before giving a little shrug. "You know Mom. My life is veering off course, and she's the only one who can fix my GPS." She rolled her eyes. "In other words, nothing new." She crossed her arms and fixed Wyatt with a stern look. "But you, my dear brother. Spill."

"I have no idea what you're referring to." Wyatt casually downed the rest of his water. When Bonnie continued to stare at him, he gave her a subtle shrug.

She threw the cap from her own bottle at him. "Oh really? Let's see if I have this right." She held up a finger for each of her points. "First, you brought a date to Gran's birthday party when none of us knew you were seeing anyone. Second, there seemed to actually be something there between you two." When Wyatt started to object, Bonnie shook her head and continued. "Third, Violet strongly dislikes Chrissy, which puts a big plus in the Chrissy column as far as I'm concerned. And fourth, apparently Gran really wants Chrissy to go to the family reunion."

Had Gran gone to see all of her grandchildren to have a discussion about Chrissy? He didn't know if that qualified as obsessive or crazy.

This was like a flashback to when he was with Ashley. Somehow every member of the family felt they should give input on his love life.

"Truthfully?" Wyatt paused and waited for Bonnie to nod that he should go on. "I think it's sad that no one else in the family has something to focus on besides my lack of a relationship."

Bonnie seemed disappointed for a moment before she crossed her arms and gave him a pointed look. "I've heard different things and figured I'd come to the source. So there's nothing at all between you and Chrissy?"

Technically, there wasn't. But the immediate rush of wishing there was hit him hard. His hesitation was apparently all Bonnie needed. She grinned triumphantly. "So why aren't you bringing her to the reunion? Come on, a romantic getaway to the beach? What's better than that?"

There was no way Wyatt would tell anyone in the family how Chrissy actually ended up at the birthday party. Anyone, that is, except for Bonnie. She was the only person who always kept his secrets. In return, he'd kept hers as well. It'd been a friendship growing up that he could rely on. She also had a way of worming information out of him.

"If I tell you, you can't breathe a word of it to anyone else. Agreed?"

"Including Gran?"

"I'm serious, Bon. Anyone. Or I'll be sure to tell

them about that field trip your junior year…"

Bonnie's face turned red, and her eyes widened. She knew full well that he would never tell her secret, but just the thought was enough to ensure her secrecy. "Okay, okay." She made a crossing mark over her heart. "So what's going on?"

Wyatt told her about how Mom had been pressuring him about bringing a date to the birthday party because it's what Gran wanted, and they needed to make her happy. He told her about asking Chrissy and then ultimately offering to pay her to accompany him.

That had Bonnie giggling again. "So you're telling me you hired a coffee barista to be your date?" When she put it that way, it sounded really lame. "You're a Tabor. The only Tabor man who isn't married, I might add. I'm pretty sure you could have dates lined up every night for the next decade if you just said the word."

He had no doubt she was right. But they'd all be lined up to go on a date with him because of his money. He was confident none of them actually cared to get to know him, and as a result, he hadn't yet convinced himself trying to date someone was worth it.

And then there was Chrissy. She was different. He wanted to give her a chance. But what if she was like all the others? He couldn't risk another relationship that ended the way it had with Ashley.

He realized then that Bonnie was just watching him with an interested look on her face. "You're never going to know if you don't try."

"And you really think bringing her to our family reunion and subjecting her to Mom and Violet is a good idea?"

Bonnie laughed at that. "Well, I think there are few people who deserve that. But," she held up a finger, "if Chrissy goes to our family reunion and *still* wants to go out with you afterward, you'll probably have a keeper."

Wyatt wanted to deny that but couldn't. Instead, he chuckled. "So I should triple my fee for the birthday party and see what happens?" It was supposed to be a joke, but he immediately sobered. The truth was, Chrissy and her family could use the money. But now that he knew her financial situation—and she knew his—any attempts to help her monetarily would be seen as charity.

His sister kicked his shin under the table, immediately making it sting. "Why don't you try asking her to go with you, dummy?"

Could he do that? Ask Chrissy to go with him to the reunion as his date? What would that say about how he felt about her? And if she said no? Just the thought made his heart drop.

If she said yes, would it be because she wanted to go with him or because of the family money? He wanted to get back in the batting cage for another round or two and try to make sense of the mess of emotions zipping through him.

Bonnie must have taken pity on him. Instead of

continuing to tease him, she leaned across the table and gently poked his arm. "You're overthinking this, big brother. If you like Chrissy and want to see if there's anything there, then ask her to go. If you don't, then skip it. In the end, it doesn't matter how much Gran wants something or how much Violet and Mom don't. What matters is what *you* want. So what are you going to do?"

Wyatt jabbed a thumb toward the batting cages. "I'm going back in there until the answer comes to me."

"In other words, you want me to tell Dad you're going to need a week or two off from work."

"Haha, cute." Wyatt reached his leg beneath the small table until his foot connected with her chair. He easily pushed it back until Bonnie could no longer comfortably reach the table.

Laughing, they both stood, and Wyatt tossed his empty bottle into a recycling bin. "I really should get back to work, though. This was fun, Bon. Let's do it again sooner than later."

"You've got it." Bonnie gave him a hug. "I won't say a word, but if you need to talk anything out, you know where I live." With another smile and a wave, she headed out.

Wyatt changed t-shirts back at his office and tried to focus on the pile of paperwork that taunted him—one of his least favorite parts of his job. Getting through it, however, proved nearly impossible because he couldn't think about anything but Chrissy.

He was still waffling between whether he should run before he developed true feelings for her or call her up and invite her to the reunion. With only a few days left, it's not like he had a lot of time left to decide.

~*~

The next day, Wyatt strongly considered skipping coffee and going to work early. No matter how many times he thought about Chrissy—or tried to convince himself that he needed to walk away from her before he got in too deep—he pictured her smile. The second he did that, their moments together flooded his memory and all he wanted to do was see her again.

What if she wasn't interested in him at all? What if she laughed when he invited her to go with him? Or worse yet, what if she was interested, and it was only because of his financial position? The fact she'd had no idea where he worked in the beginning made him feel a little better. After all, he was pretty sure they had a connection before he'd told her.

If he didn't ask her, would he regret it? He immediately knew that he would. It was that realization that led him straight to the coffee shop. But upon entering, Chrissy was nowhere to be seen. Hopefully Emma wasn't sick again. He got in line, ordered his coffee, and was about to text her to see if she was okay when she hurried in.

Instead of her normal jeans and t-shirt, she wore black slacks and a pretty blue long-sleeved blouse. He realized that she wasn't wearing most of her rings and the sleeves came down to her wrists, effectively covering the tattoo.

Her attire looked perfect on her small frame, but strands of her hair had worked themselves loose from the clip at the back of her head. She looked frazzled, and the fact she was in such a hurry to reach the back room that she nearly ran into him only confirmed it. He reached out and caught her before she tripped over his shoe.

Chrissy looked up and gasped. "I'm so sorry!" She gripped his upper arms to regain her balance, and the feel of her palms against his skin completely distracted him. She let go way sooner than he wanted her to.

"Are you okay? I hope Emma's feeling all right."

"What?" She looked confused for a minute before her eyes widened a little. "Oh! No, it's not that. Emma's fine." She lowered her voice as much as she could and still be heard over the din of the coffee shop. "I had an interview first thing this morning. I was supposed to be back twenty minutes ago." She glanced at an employee who was handling the morning crowd by herself. "I need to get back there. I'm sorry I missed you earlier."

Was she looking for a new job or a second one? He wished he could ask her more about it now, but this wasn't the time or the place. "Are you available for lunch?"

"I can't. I need to work through lunch to make

up for this morning." She placed a hand on his arm again and gave it a gentle squeeze. "I'll talk to you later, okay?"

"Sure." Wyatt watched as she disappeared into the back and returned with an apron. She rolled up her sleeves and got to work. He hated the idea that Chrissy might be getting a second job.

She handed him his coffee with a tired smile. He gave her a wave and left, unable to get her off his mind. Everything about her spoke of a woman who was exhausted and stressed. Wyatt probably ought to let it go, but that was never one of his strengths. As the day wore on, he formulated a plan, even if he had a feeling Chrissy was going to dislike his idea.

That evening, without calling first, he headed over to Chrissy's house. He rang the doorbell, and a few moments later, Sarah answered the door, a look of surprise on her face. "Good evening."

"Hello. I'm so sorry to bother you. Is Chrissy available? I just wanted to speak to her for a few minutes."

Sarah studied him, curiosity shining in her eyes. "Let me get her. Would you like to come inside?"

Wyatt slid his hands into the pockets of his jeans and gave a subtle nod. "Thank you." He took two steps through the front door and waited, uncertain how Chrissy would view his unexpected visit. When she came in, he took in her baggy knit shorts and the t-shirt that was at least two sizes too big. Part of her hair was pulled back with stray strands dangling near her ears. It was all he could do to keep his hands in his pockets and not reach out to see if it was as soft as it looked.

She appeared uncertain as she approached. "Hey, Wyatt. Is everything okay?"

He tipped his head toward the front door. "Do you have a few minutes to talk?"

Chrissy looked toward the living room where her mom and sister were sitting. Was she looking for a reason to say no? She finally shrugged. "Sure."

Wyatt held the door open for her and then closed it securely behind them. He waited for her to take a seat on one of the three steps that led from the porch to the cracked sidewalk below before joining her. The steps weren't quite wide enough for them to sit next to each other, so he sat on a step one lower than her. They both naturally turned to face each other, their knees nearly touching.

He'd been trying to decide all day where he should begin the conversation. Not knowing how much time they had, he dove right in. "How'd the interview go?"

Chrissy cringed. "Not well. The hours are flexible, so I was hoping for weekends. They want nights. I don't think I can handle six to midnight and still work at the coffee shop. Not if I want to stay awake, anyway." She gave a short laugh. "But we'll see. Maybe if I work that shift for a while, I can move to weekends later."

"And what? Work every waking hour?" That wasn't healthy for anyone. "Has Emma not had any luck job hunting?"

She shook her head and lowered her voice. "She's just now feeling well enough to start. She interviewed at one place but when they heard why she'd had to give up this last job, I think it scared them. Nothing like worrying about a new employee having to take off extensive time for sick leave, you know?" She sighed. "She's stressed and not in a position to deal with this right now. So if I can get a second job for a while, it'll take some of the pressure off her."

"What about you?"

"I can handle it." Chrissy's spine straightened, and she lifted her chin as though daring him to contradict her.

He had no doubt she could, but at what cost? "I've watched my dad work himself to death all my life, Chrissy. I'd wake up in the morning, and he'd have been at work for hours. I would hear him come home again long after I went to bed. And it was rare to have a weekend when he was home even for part of it. He'll deny it to his dying day, but it's taken a toll on his health. On our family." He rested a hand on her arm for a brief moment. "I don't want to see you entering that kind of lifestyle."

"What other choice do I have?" Her whisper was fierce, and unshed tears made her eyes glisten.

This was as good of a time as any. Wyatt took in a long breath before releasing it slowly. "So I've thought about this all day. At first, I was going to offer to give you some money to help, and I knew you'd turn me down flat." She raised her brows and gave him a look that more than verified that hunch. "Then I thought I'd offer to loan you the money, but knew you'd say no to that, too."

"Okay…" Chrissy looked confused. "Where are you going with this?"

"Gran desperately wants you to come to the family reunion."

One corner of her mouth lifted in a half smile. "I know. She sent me an invitation herself."

Now it was Wyatt's turn to be surprised. Wow, Gran had a lot of nerve. "I didn't realize that." He paused. "Well, I thought maybe we could take our arrangement for the birthday party and extend it. What if you go as my date to the reunion, and I pay you for your trouble?" He told her the amount he had in mind, and Chrissy started to stand up.

Wyatt reached for her hand and held it in his, encouraging her to stay. "Hopefully it'll be enough to keep you guys going until Emma can find another job. You won't have to work your fingers to the bone, and it'll make Gran happy. Not to mention get her off both of our backs." When Chrissy tossed him a curious look, he elaborated. "On Sunday, she tried to persuade me to get you to the reunion one way or the other." He shrugged. "She's a hard woman to say no to."

"I get that about your Gran. Trust me. But I'm not taking your money. I'm definitely not taking that much money." She ran her fingers through a small section of her hair, apparently only then wondering about her appearance. Her cheeks turned pink, and she took the clip out, shaking her head to try to get her hair to fall into place. Several strands caught on the earring of her left ear.

Wyatt carefully used a finger to sweep them away, then lingered near her ear just a moment longer than he needed to.

Chrissy blinked at him. "Your Gran may want me there. I'm pretty sure Violet would do about anything to make sure I'm not. The way I see it, the votes cancel each other out."

"I thought you'd turn down the money. So I have a plan B. What about a job for Emma? At the country club, I mean. There are several openings, and I think Emma would be perfect for one of them." Chrissy looked stunned. "I'd love for her to drop by anytime next week and apply if she's interested."

Her mouth opened slightly before closing it again. "So you want me to go to your family reunion in exchange for getting Emma a job?"

Ugh, he was completely making a mess out of all of this. "Let me start over." He paused for a moment. "There are several job openings at the country club, and I immediately thought about Emma. The schedules are super flexible, and the boss happens to know the situation so wouldn't mind if she needs to take some time off for health reasons." He smiled, but Chrissy didn't return it. "The job opportunity has nothing to do with the family reunion."

"You're serious."

"I am." He bumped her knee with his. "And if a certain sister of hers insists on finding a second job, I'm pretty sure there's one that requires weekends only." Wyatt would rather she didn't get a second job, but if she was going to be stubborn about it, at least she wouldn't be working nights, too.

His comment earned him a small smile.

"I'll let Emma know. Thank you, Wyatt."

"You're welcome." Wyatt couldn't get over the way her smile went right to her brown eyes, bringing out gold specks of color. "As for the reunion, what happens if I cast my vote for you to come along?"

"I...I..." She wrapped her arms around her knees and pulled them closer to her chest. "I have to work on Friday."

"You can go home and change, I'll pick you up, and we can drive over afterward." He tried not to hold out too much hope that she might agree to go. "You get off work at four, right? Corpus Christi is just three hours away. We could get something to eat from a drive-through and be there before it gets dark."

"Your family doesn't need me crashing the reunion." Chrissy got up and brushed her shorts off.

Wyatt followed suit, reached out, and cupped her elbow. "You realize you're not crashing if you come as my date, right?"

"I couldn't do that. It's way too last minute."

"Trust me when I say there are plenty of rooms at the resort my parents have reserved. There are always way more than we need, but they buy the place out for the long weekend anyway." Her hesitation had his heart racing in panic. He'd enjoyed spending time with her over the last couple of weeks. Despite his own hang-ups about relationships, he'd been convinced there was something between them. Maybe it was all just an illusion. See, and this was exactly why he'd avoided this type of situation in the first place.

"Wyatt?"

"Yeah?" He tried to act casual as she seemed to search his face.

"If it means that much to your Gran, maybe I could drive up for the day or something to say hello."

Wyatt smiled when he realized she'd completely misunderstood him. A breeze came through and blew some hair across her lips. She brushed it away, but he couldn't take his focus from her mouth as she gently drew her lip in beneath her top front teeth.

"I don't want you to go for Gran. Or to tick my sister off, although that would be a bonus." He reached for her hand and held it gently in his. "I want you to come as my date because I'd enjoy spending some more time with you."

"I don't know…" Chrissy's eyes went to their joined hands. "I'm not sure it's a good idea to go away for that long. What if something happens here?"

"Then we will drop everything and drive back." He threaded their fingers together. "It'll be fun. Or at least an adventure. What do you say?" This was either the start of something amazing, or he was just setting himself up for disappointment and regret. He wasn't sure if he was more hopeful or nervous as he waited for her answer.

A tentative smile lifted the corners of her mouth. "I've always wanted to see the ocean."

Chapter Ten

Chrissy worried leaving Emma and Mom behind would result in a stressful trip. It'd taken everything in her to not embarrass herself by crying as she got into the Jeep and gave her family one last wave. Now that Clearwater was disappearing in the rearview mirror, the tension began to dissipate from her shoulders.

When Chrissy had second-guessed herself over and over again about agreeing to go with Wyatt, her family kept telling her she was doing the right thing. Mom asked when the last time was that Chrissy had done something for herself. She'd been ready to volley instance after instance right back at her. Several moments of silence later, Chrissy had finally admitted she didn't know.

When Chrissy realized she had no excuses or reason to get out of the reunion, she relaxed into the leather seat of Wyatt's Jeep and watched through her window as the trees zipped by. This was good for her. In fact, after all the stress of the last few years, maybe this was exactly what she needed. Having the most handsome man she'd ever known sitting in the next seat over certainly didn't hurt things, either.

Wyatt glanced at her. He'd picked her up at the house wearing a pair of tan cargo shorts, a Star Wars t-shirt, and a welcoming smile. Despite his mixed feelings about the reunion and some of the cautionary tales he'd told her, he seemed ready to get away for a couple of days.

Chrissy, on the other hand, kept ping-ponging between being excited about spending time with Wyatt and nervous about what it all meant. That evening while she waited for Wyatt to pick her up, Emma insisted it was clear he was falling for Chrissy. The very idea had her heart banging painfully against her ribs.

She seriously doubted Emma was right. But what if she were falling for him?

Wyatt reached for a bottle of water in the cup holder between them, took a drink, and put it back. For half a second, Chrissy thought he might reach over and hold her hand. The disappointment that hit when he didn't reminded her that she needed to get a grip.

Whether or not there was something here between them remained to be seen. Either way, a reunion where she'd be surrounded by his extended family was not likely the place she'd find out.

She may as well focus on the good food and her

first experience at the beach.

"So the resort is close to the coast?"

"You can see the ocean from many of the rooms." Wyatt flashed her a smile. "And you can go out and walk right down the beach. It's an amazing location. My family has a standing reservation for this week every year. I have an aunt who comes from Canada, and an uncle in Hawaii who makes the trip."

"Wow, so you have family that wasn't at your grandmother's birthday party?"

Wyatt laughed loudly at that. "Oh, you have no idea. But you're right, with Gran's party, we've got back-to-back family reunions of sorts. But there will be a lot more people this weekend, trust me."

"That's wonderful everyone takes the time out of their busy lives to gather together like that." Her voice carried a wistfulness that surprised even her. "You really are lucky to have such a large extended family."

"For better or worse, I know you're right." He passed a slower vehicle on the highway before getting back in the right lane again. He smiled at her. "I still can't believe you've never seen the ocean."

"Mom always wanted to take us. But as kids, Emma got sick easily. Most of our vacations—few and far between that they were—revolved around staying at home or maybe a hotel in Austin or Dallas. I guess time just got away from us…" A pang of guilt hit her, and she tried to push it away. Neither Mom or Emma would want her to feel bad. Instead, they would want her to have fun and come back with a full report on her experience.

They made a stop halfway through to stretch their legs and grab something to eat in the Jeep. Chrissy enjoyed watching the scenery change as they traveled across East Texas to the Gulf of Mexico. Corpus Christi was interesting to look at as they went through. Chrissy kept her eyes peeled for her first sign of the ocean.

"You see that gray there along the horizon?" Wyatt pointed out the driver's side, and she nodded. "That's the Corpus Christi Bay. We'll follow it down, go across a long causeway, and then the resort is on Mustang Island."

Chrissy listened to him point out different highlights as they continued on their drive. Her favorite, however, was definitely the causeway. They were halfway across when Chrissy remembered her mom and sister. She took several pictures and recorded a short video to show them.

Wyatt lowered the windows so they could breathe in the ocean air as they continued on their trek. They hadn't gone far when he took an exit.

"Oh, are we close to the resort?" Chrissy scanned the buildings ahead.

"Not quite." He continued to drive until they approached a clearing. From there, she could easily see the ocean in front of her. "I didn't think your first visit to the beach should be within the chaos of my family's reunion." He parked the car near a trail that led down to the beach below. "What do you say? We have some time before we have to be at the resort."

"Are you serious?" Chrissy's gaze followed the trail to the pale sand beyond. There were only a few people strolling along the beach or walking near the waves. She wasn't about to turn his offer down. "Let's go!"

Wyatt chuckled as he got out of the Jeep and led the way.

It took more energy than Chrissy thought it would to walk across the sand. The sound of the waves hitting the beach filled the air. She took in a deep breath, certain she would never forget the way it smelled here. While she didn't think it was much cooler here than it was back in Clearwater, there was a breeze coming off the water that felt amazing.

She paused only inches from where the sand became wet. Mesmerized, she watched as the waves crept closer only to finally cover the sand nearby in a frothy mix of foam and water. Then it seemed to race itself back out again.

"You should take your sandals off."

Wyatt's words broke into Chrissy's thoughts. She turned to see him doing just that a few feet away. "We have time?"

"Absolutely."

She didn't have to be told twice. The sand warmed the bottoms of her feet as it pressed itself into the spaces between her toes.

Wyatt held a hand out. "Give me your phone and then go stand just where the waves will cover your feet.

I'll take a few pictures for you."

Chrissy grinned, pulled up her camera application, and handed the phone to him. She carefully traversed the few feet until the sand became wet and cool.

The next wave approached and swirled around her ankles. She was surprised to feel the sand shift around her feet as they sank and became covered. She looked up to find Wyatt smiling at her as he looked at her phone. She'd have to send a few of these to Mom and Emma. She grinned as she held her arms out to her side and then waved.

The water began to recede. Wyatt brought the phone down and gave her a thumbs-up. "I think I got several good ones. You'll have to check when we get in the Jeep since it's hard to see the screen out here in the sun."

She met him halfway and accepted the phone, slipping it into her back pocket again. She was glad she wore capris today because it made it easy to splash in the waves. "Thank you."

"You're welcome." He glanced in the direction of the sun. "Let's go for a walk before it starts to get dark."

Chrissy readily agreed. He led the way toward the ocean until the waves lapped at her shins, and then they began to follow the coastline. If she didn't have her keys and phone in her pocket, she'd be tempted to chase the waves out and then race to see if she could beat them back in again. She decided she'd find time to do that before the weekend was over.

Meanwhile, she enjoyed the way the waves caressed the skin on her feet and lower legs every time they came in and out. Several times, if they'd paused to enjoy the sensation, she'd have to lift her feet out of the sand where they'd become buried.

Wyatt cleared his throat. "I need to make a point of coming out here sometime when we aren't having the family reunion. I forgot how peaceful this can be." He chuckled. "You'll see what I mean tomorrow. You'll have plenty of opportunity to go down to the beach by the resort, but there will be very little peace."

Chrissy stopped walked and turned to face him. "What did your family do for vacations?"

"My parents preferred the mountains. We went skiing a lot. Not that there's anything wrong with that." He spotted something, stooped, and picked it up. He motioned for her to open her hand.

She did so, and he dropped a small shell into her palm.

"There, now you have a souvenir of your first trip to the beach."

Chrissy studied the shell, noting the little details etched into it, and smiled. It didn't matter what happened at the reunion itself—or even whether there really was something going on between her and Wyatt—this time at the beach made the trip entirely worth it.

She raised her gaze to his. "Thank you. For the shell and for this." The only sound she heard was the low rush of the waves around them. "I had no idea how badly I needed to get away until now. This place is incredible. I don't know how people live so close to the ocean and don't just spend all their time right here."

Chrissy could picture herself owning a beach house. She imagined waking up on a lazy Saturday, walking barefoot down the beach to the place where a pair of lounge chairs waited. She'd ease herself into one of those chairs and bask in the sound of the waves. Suddenly, Wyatt was there, too, sitting in the other chair. It was as natural to find him there as it was for him to reach for her hand and press a kiss to it.

She shook herself and blinked at the setting sun. Good grief, she had to get a grip on herself. Heat suffused her cheeks, and she hoped it just looked like the warm air was getting to her. The last thing she needed to do was start imagining herself with Wyatt in the future. Certainly not in a happily-ever-after capacity, anyway, no matter how natural it'd felt in her daydream.

She wished she knew what it all meant. Was it possible to keep an open mind about it while simultaneously maintaining a protective barrier around her own heart? What she needed to do was keep it casual, enjoy getting away for the weekend, and keep reminding herself that she and Wyatt were way too different for anything to really work out between them.

~*~

Wyatt watched as Chrissy's face slowly transformed from relaxed and happy to something more akin to pensive. She was staring at the horizon away from the water with a small frown on her face. Her cheeks had gotten a little pink. He should've thought to bring a bottle of water for each of them to take on the walk. He hadn't figured they'd stroll as far as they did. In fact, they'd better start heading back so it wouldn't be too dark to find their shoes or his Jeep.

He reached for her hand. He'd intended to only touch it to bring her attention back to the present. But the moment their skin met, he grasped her hand in his as though he had no control over it himself.

Chrissy's skin felt cool against his. That broke through her thoughts, and her gaze shifted to their joined hands and then up to his face.

"You okay?"

She nodded. "Yeah." She shrugged and glanced down at her feet. It looked like she tried to shift her weight when surprise flitted across her face. "Wow, those waves buried my feet fast. I guess that's why you don't build sandcastles or leave anything near the water."

Wyatt pulled his own feet out of the sand. "Just don't let them sink too far or the hermit crabs will pinch your toes," he said jokingly.

"What?!" Chrissy jumped into the air and then hurriedly washed the sand off her feet in the next wave that reached them.

Still holding onto her hand, Wyatt couldn't help

but chuckle. "I'm teasing you, Chrissy."

She smacked his arm and pinned him with an accusing look. "That's not funny."

"It was a little."

Chrissy tried to keep a stern look on her face but soon dissolved into giggles of her own. The sound washed over him, every bit as refreshing and memorable as the ocean waves themselves. He fought the temptation to put his other arm around her waist and draw her closer. He was succeeding, too, until she looked up at him with those gorgeous brown eyes. Her lips parted slightly, immediately drawing his attention.

He ought to steer her back in the direction they'd come, but his feet wouldn't move. The distance between them evaporated, though he wasn't sure which of them moved first.

Wyatt leaned down until his lips brushed against hers in a brief kiss. He was going to step back, but her soft sigh had him moving in to kiss her again. Just before he felt the warmth of her lips, she straightened, and her face moved away from his.

His heart stalled and then raced like a runaway train. "What's wrong?"

Chrissy gripped his arms for another moment before dropping her hands. The pink in her cheeks was just barely visible in the fading sun. "I can't... you may end up being Emma's boss... It'd be weird," she finished lamely. Her chin fell as she clasped her hands together in an obvious sign of discomfort. "I'm sorry."

There was no doubt she was right, but Wyatt's

throat tightened with disappointment. Their kiss was so short, he might have imagined it. But it'd been long enough to prove they had some serious chemistry there.

Maybe he shouldn't have pressed her to come to the reunion with him. As much as he wanted to regret doing so, he couldn't. The look on her face as she experienced the ocean for the first time made it all worthwhile.

Wyatt reached out to touch her arm but stopped himself. "No, I'm the one who should be sorry." He cleared his throat, uncertain what to say. He gestured toward the waves and then in the direction of the sunset. "I blame the ambiance." To his relief, she gave a little laugh. "Come on, we'd better be getting back before it's too dark to find our shoes."

She seemed relieved for the change in subject. They walked along the beach in near silence, allowing his thoughts to all but scream in his head.

Was it wrong to want to kiss Chrissy again? She clearly regretted it. She seemed like the type to slap first and demand an apology later if he were to try it again. Knowing his family, it was unlikely he and Chrissy would get any time alone.

That was for the best. He had a feeling it would be way too easy to allow himself to fall for Chrissy.

Chapter Eleven

So much for keeping things casual. Chrissy had no idea what to say to Wyatt right now. He'd kissed her. It had her heart soaring higher than it should have for such a brief moment in time. She'd wanted him to kiss her again, too, until her common sense took over. Chrissy suppressed a groan as her mind wandered to all the ways this was going to complicate the weekend. They hadn't talked about it, but she'd assumed the public displays of affection rules from the birthday party applied here. Holding hands only when necessary. Yeah, pretty sure kissing went a bit beyond that.

She remembered what he'd said about all the family members attending the reunion. If there really were so many people, there's no way she and Wyatt would even be in a situation where they'd be tempted to kiss again. See, it was all a moot point. Keep to group activities, and they'd be just fine.

Relief collided with disappointment, which was

completely ridiculous. It was one kiss with a guy that was completely wrong for her and likely her sister's future boss.

Agreeing to go to this shindig was a stupid, stupid mistake.

"The resort is just up ahead."

Chrissy stared as the giant building grew larger the closer they got. It looked like something out of a travel magazine from some exotic country. She had no idea there was such a place right here in Texas. Waterfalls cascaded down the sign welcoming them as they drove through the twenty-foot gates and followed a paved road to the circular driveway out front.

The Jeep had barely come to a stop before doormen approached. They wore slacks and long-sleeved dress shirts with the resort logo on them. Wyatt got out and unlocked the back. The men collected their luggage and headed for the impressive front entrance of the resort.

Chrissy opened her door to find Wyatt waiting to hold it for her. She slid out of the seat and slipped past him. They were close enough for her to catch a whiff of his aftershave, and she ignored the instinct to linger for another one. Seriously, no guy should be able to walk along the coast in the heat like he did and still smell that good.

She felt his hand lightly touch her lower back as they walked past various topiaries to the towering door. Two more doormen opened it for them.

Chrissy took in the flowers, crystal, highly

polished floor, and plush carpet. It made the country club look like a cardboard box. She tried to guess how much renting this place for the weekend must've set Wyatt's parents back. She couldn't imagine having even a sliver of that kind of money.

Wyatt led the way to the front desk. He'd clearly been here many times before and didn't seem phased by the décor. It only served as a reminder of how very different they were. If he hadn't come into the coffee shop, Chrissy was certain they never would've crossed paths anywhere else.

There was no way she would fit in here. She was trying to figure out how she could get back home without Wyatt having to miss his reunion by taking her when Violet walked in. There was a flash of surprise in her eyes before she composed herself, lifted her chin, and approached.

Escaping was going to be next to impossible now. Chrissy reminded herself that her mom and sister would insist she stay. She could almost hear Emma telling her that this would be her one chance to feel like a princess in a castle.

Violet gave her brother a hug and Chrissy a fake smile. "I'm so glad the two of you could make it. Are you just checking in?"

Wyatt accepted two sheets of paper. He signed one and handed Chrissy the other to sign. A quick glance told her it was just a paper outlining responsibility for the room. She didn't have to pay for it, but of course it would make sense that each occupant would sign one of those agreements. Especially if the room was even remotely decorated as nicely as the rest of the resort...

Wyatt handed over the signed papers and turned to Violet. "Yes, we just got here."

Violet's eyes followed their every move. "Wow, you're staying in separate rooms." Her brows rose high enough to disappear behind her bangs. She said nothing else, but the implication was still there.

Wyatt didn't flinch. "You know how Gran is. She might pretend, but she'd never be okay with Chrissy and me sleeping in the same room."

He tossed Violet a look of warning. Did Violet just assume everyone was sleeping together, or was she trying to get on his nerves? Chrissy was glad he was handling the conversation well because she, on the other hand, was busy mentally counting the number of tiny lightbulbs in the chandelier. Thankfully, neither of the siblings seemed to expect her to add to the exchange.

A glance at Violet's face told her that Wyatt's sister wasn't happy with his response, but she didn't feel like she could say anything else, either.

A bellhop appeared with their luggage on a rolling cart. "If you two will follow me, I'll show you to your rooms."

Thankful for the distraction, they proceeded to the elevator and up to the third floor. The bellhop opened door 312 and motioned for Chrissy to enter. "This is your room, miss."

Chrissy's eyes widened as she took in the space that would qualify as an apartment anywhere else. With a small kitchenette, a luxurious bathroom complete with a garden tub, and a giant king-sized bed, Chrissy was confident she could comfortably live there.

The bellhop put her luggage on a small table. He picked up a piece of paper from a desk in one corner and turned with a smile. "Here's a schedule for tomorrow. Breakfast begins at five and is served through ten. If there's anything you need, just pick up the phone and dial zero. We're happy to help."

"Thank you." Chrissy took the paper from him. Before she had the chance to offer a tip—and she had no idea what amount would be appropriate—Wyatt stepped forward and slipped some money into the man's hand.

He bowed slightly and motioned back to the door. "I'll show you to your room, sir. It's right across the hall."

Wyatt smiled at Chrissy. "I'll see you in the morning for breakfast?"

"Sure. What time?"

He thought a moment. "Are you an early bird or do you like to sleep in? There are people here who will do both, which is why breakfast is served for so long."

"Early bird most of the time. But I think having the chance to sleep in a little would be nice."

He smiled. "In that case, how about I knock on your door at nine?"

"That'll be great." She looked around the room.

"I'll see you tomorrow."

"Good night, Chrissy." He paused a moment before smiling again then followed the bellhop outside. The door closed, blocking her view of him.

Chrissy allowed herself to fall backward onto the large bed. A groan escaped her lips. "Oh, yeah." She wondered how badly everyone would think of her if she just slept through the day tomorrow. Whatever kind of mattress this was, it was going on the top of Chrissy's bucket list of things to own one day.

She was still holding the schedule and took time to look at the activities lined up for tomorrow. After breakfast was beach volleyball, followed by a scavenger hunt. It sounded like basic shorts and a t-shirt would be good for that. Hopefully she could just observe and cheer because volleyball was never one of the sports she'd taken to.

It was almost ten o'clock. Not really all that late, but she was already exhausted. She changed into a pair of knit shorts and t-shirt before collapsing on the bed again. She called Mom who put her on speaker so that Emma could hear the conversation as well.

An hour later, she'd finished telling them about the drive, how fancy the resort was, and her trip to the coast. The one thing she refused to mention was the kiss. They ended the call with Chrissy promising to take and send more pictures.

Fifteen minutes later, she crawled under the covers, relaxed between the satin sheets, and tried not to stress about the unknowns of tomorrow.

She'd only be there for about thirty-six hours. That wasn't so long. She could handle pretending to be Wyatt's girlfriend, especially if it made his grandmother happy. Enjoying the amazing amenities at this fancy resort was another perk. She just had to keep her game face on.

Oh, and make sure she and Wyatt didn't kiss again.

~*~

Wyatt stepped onto the back deck and took in a deep breath of ocean air. Much better. Breakfast had been fine, but there'd been something about all the people milling around that made him feel claustrophobic.

Chrissy had been exceptionally quiet during breakfast as well. She'd sat beside him, exchanged pleasantries, and happily spoke to several members of his extended family. But there was something about her demeanor that made him wonder if she was more unsure than she let on. Was it because of their kiss? More likely it was because of the crowd of people she didn't know. Just because he couldn't quit thinking about being close at the beach didn't mean she was having the same problem.

He glanced at her as she picked up a brightly-colored beach blanket from the folded pile on the deck and tucked it under one arm. Over the other shoulder was a large canvas bag filled with an umbrella, a sunhat, and some other items he couldn't quite see.

Chrissy pulled the sunhat out and put it on her head. The cream-colored fabric did a good job of blocking her face from the sun. Between the hat, the brown shorts, and floral-patterned sleeveless shirt she was wearing, she looked like she was meant to be on the beach.

They made their way down the well-kept path that led from the steps of the deck halfway to the beach. Chrissy glanced at him. "I have to admit, I was surprised when you said you'd be playing volleyball."

Wyatt chuckled. "It's an acquired sport. My sisters all played it growing up, so I did, too." Ahead, people were gathering near the volleyball nets and reserving places to sit.

"Is it super competitive?"

"We'll keep track of points to see which team wins. As for how competitive everyone is, it entirely depends on which team you're talking about." Wyatt flashed her a grin.

"I'm glad I decided to just sit on the sidelines and watch." She shifted her bag on her shoulder.

Wyatt instinctively reached for it. She seemed surprised but allowed him to carry it for her. "Good idea to bring an umbrella. I hope you put sunscreen in here, too."

"I did." She held one arm out. "I don't get a whole lot of sun. I'd rather not go home looking like a boiled lobster."

He led the way to a spot close enough to the

volleyball nets to see, but far enough away that Chrissy shouldn't have to worry about stray balls. They worked together to spread out the large blanket. She took her bag from him and set it down before lowering herself to sit on one edge. Immediately, she kicked her sandals off and buried her feet in the sand. Her toes, complete with purple nails, peeked out like colorful little seashells.

Wyatt had never really thought of feet as attractive until now. Then again, he couldn't think of anything about Chrissy that wasn't beautiful.

Realizing he was still staring at her toes, Wyatt blinked to clear his head and focus on his uncle who was relating details about which team he was going to be on.

The games weren't starting for another half hour, so Wyatt took the opportunity to sit beside Chrissy and relax for a few minutes.

Lucy stopped at their towel, crouched down with her Canon in hand, and snapped several pictures. Chrissy's head lifted. There was only a momentary look of surprise on her face before she smiled brightly for the camera. Lucy then focused on Chrissy's feet, her toes still sticking out of the sand.

"You're not wasting any time this morning," Wyatt commented.

His sister only shrugged as she snapped some more photos. "The candid pictures are always the best. The one time I don't have my camera out is the time I'll miss the best shot of the weekend." It was all said while looking through the eyepiece.

"Well, don't forget to take part in the events and not just photograph them."

Lucy stuck her tongue out at Wyatt, and he returned the gesture. They both smiled as she continued to canvas the area and moved away to shoot something else.

"She seems really nice." Chrissy put her hands on the blanket behind her and leaned back. "She's right about candid pictures."

"Yeah, Lucy's great. Even though I think she spends too much time behind her camera during the reunion."

"The problem with being the photographer is that you're never in the pictures."

"Exactly." Wyatt removed his own sandals and relished the feel of the sun on his skin. "She's good at what she does, though. We keep telling her she should open her own studio, but she says it'll turn a fun hobby into a stressful job." He lifted a palm full of sand and let it sift through his fingers. "You'll get to see the pictures. She usually creates a slideshow and sends everyone a copy. I'll make sure you get one."

"I appreciate that." Chrissy withdrew a folded piece of paper from one of her back pockets. She opened it and laid it on the blanket, smoothing out the creases. "Which other events do you participate in?"

Wyatt took in the list. "I usually help my nieces and nephews with the scavenger hunt." Wow, they'd really packed the two days in with more activities than usual. His parents were always doing their best to make everyone happy, which was impossible. "Everything's optional, though, except for dinner this evening. A lot of people will choose a couple activities per day and spend the rest of the time splashing and relaxing on the beach. Don't feel like you have to do anything you don't want to do." He was having a difficult time gauging what she was interested in.

She nodded thoughtfully. "If you don't mind, I'd like to help with the scavenger hunt, then maybe hang out at the beach this afternoon. I definitely want to be there for the bonfire tonight after dinner, though." She folded the paper again and slipped it back into her pocket. "I haven't been to a bonfire since my senior year of high school."

"That sounds good." He liked that she wanted to stay for the volleyball games. Would she cheer for him and his team? It shouldn't make a difference, but it did.

He was also glad she decided to stay because he didn't want to leave her completely on her own with Violet and his mother wandering around. He could keep an eye on her and make sure some of the more…nosy…family members left her alone. The primary reason for sticking together, of course.

At least that's what he kept telling himself.

Chapter Twelve

Chrissy closed her eyes and sprayed some extra sunscreen on her face. She used her hands to massage it into her skin, hoping she hadn't missed any white streaks. It was too bad she hadn't brought a mirror.

Sure, I'll remember one the next time I go to the beach and watch my fake boyfriend play volleyball. She almost smiled at her sarcastic line of thinking. Most women might have a compact in their bag, but since Chrissy almost never wore makeup, it wasn't exactly on her priority list. She applied more sunscreen on her arms and legs, being sure to cover any exposed skin. Once that was done, she tugged her sunhat back on and turned her attention to the game.

Wyatt, along with the other five members of his team, stood ready. Someone on the opposite side of the net served the ball, and everyone jumped into action. Chrissy wished she understood the rules of the game. All she knew was that someone served the ball and then everyone else tried to keep it from hitting the sand. Right now, Wyatt's team was ahead by three points.

Of course, it'd been hard to concentrate on all aspects of the game anyway once Wyatt had shed his t-shirt. It wasn't like he was the only bare-chested guy out there.

If she hadn't stopped their kiss the other night, she would've known what it would be like to be held in those strong arms of his.

She shook the stupid thought from her head with frustration. She had no right to be thinking anything like that, not when she was the one who drew the line in the sand. Even now, Chrissy stood by her decision. She took her cell phone out and snapped several photos of the goings-on around her. She managed to get two of Wyatt, not that she was trying, including an action shot as he jumped into the air to block the ball.

Knowing her family would want to see more photo proof of her mini vacation, Chrissy took several selfies showing the sandy beach in the background. She sent one of them to Mom and Emma along with beach ball and umbrella emojis.

A shadow fell over her moments before someone joined her on the towel. Chrissy tilted her head to find Wyatt's youngest sister, Bonnie, with a young baby in her arms. The little boy looked to be about six months old. Chrissy didn't think Bonnie had children, but then she'd met so many people, she could easily be mistaken. Still, his red hair and green eyes didn't remotely resemble Bonnie's features.

Bonnie smiled warmly. "I was hoping I'd run into you. Are you having fun?"

"I am, thank you." Chrissy adjusted her sunhat so that she could see Bonnie easier. "How about you guys?" The baby reached out and grabbed the brim of her sunhat. She laughed as she carefully worked it loose from his grip.

Bonnie kissed the little boy's cheek and switched him to the knee furthest from Chrissy. "We are. There's lots to see, isn't there, Gunner?" She smoothed his hair back and shifted again to make sure he was in the shade her body created.

Chrissy got the umbrella out of her bag, opened it, and held it out.

"Thank you. I should've thought to bring one myself but having Gunner with me was a last-minute change." The baby fiddled with the loop at the base of the handle. "I'm his nanny. I was supposed to have this weekend off, but his dad was called away to work, so I brought him with me. Although my parents weren't thrilled."

Chrissy wanted to ask Bonnie why her parents wouldn't want her to bring the baby but figured it wasn't her business. "It's great you were able to make it."

"I'm glad we could, too. It wasn't easy, though. My car is in the shop, so I had to hitch a ride with Lucy's family. They're staying later Sunday than we can." She cringed. "I was wondering, if you don't mind, could we hitch a ride back to Clearwater with you and Wyatt? I have Gunner's car seat in my room."

"I can't speak for Wyatt, but I don't mind in the least."

"Awesome! I appreciate that." She nodded toward the volleyball court. "I don't want Gunner to get sunburned or overheated, but we had to come down for a while and catch some of the action."

They watched the volleyball game in silence until Wyatt's team scored another point and cheered, giving each other high fives or fist bumps. Wyatt glanced her way, and their gazes tangled for a moment before a teammate spoke to him and pulled him back into the game.

Chrissy's heart lodged itself in her throat. She cleared it and turned back to Bonnie. "Would you normally be out there playing volleyball, too?"

"Absolutely. Usually Wyatt and I are on the same team."

"The team captain picked him first. Apparently he's in high demand, and I can see why. He plays well out there." Wyatt made another block, and Chrissy clapped with the rest of the crowd.

"If you think he's good at volleyball, you should see him on a baseball field." Bonnie tickled Gunner under the chin, eliciting an infectious belly laugh from the baby.

"I take it he was quite the jock in high school."

"You could say that." Bonnie flashed her another smile. "Good at sports, good at school, popular."

"Was it hard being several years behind him?"

"Nah. He kinda paved the way for me."

Chrissy suddenly wondered if Wyatt had met Ashley back then. Were they high school sweethearts? Or had they met later in college? The question was on the tip of her tongue before she swallowed it. Their relationship was certainly not Chrissy's concern regardless of how curious she was.

The crowd erupted in another round of applause. Chrissy glanced up quick enough to see that Wyatt's team had scored yet another point. The defeated look on the faces of the other team told her that they likely weren't going to be able to come back from behind. Wyatt's bright smile settled on her again, and Chrissy returned it without thinking twice.

Only then did she realize Bonnie was watching them with a crooked grin on her face.

"It's good to see my brother happy like this. It's been a while."

Chrissy had no idea what to say. Instead, when Gunner snatched one of her sandals off the blanket, Chrissy took advantage of the change in subject and helped Bonnie get it out of the boy's grasp. "Wow, he's got some seriously strong fingers," she said with a chuckle.

"No kidding. I'm constantly having to keep him from putting everything in his mouth." Bonnie pulled his lower lip down just enough to show two white buds on his gums. "He cut these last week, and I think he has two more coming in on top."

Chrissy watched the two interact for several moments before Gunner started to fuss.

Bonnie handed over the umbrella and stood with the baby in her arms. "That's my cue. Looks like it's time to walk around for a while before I go put this guy down for a nap. It was good to visit with you, Chrissy. By the way, nice ink."

Chrissy automatically put a hand on her tattoo. "Thank you."

"I hope we see you again later."

"Me, too." Chrissy waved and watched them disappear behind some other people. She stretched her legs out in front of her and continued to watch the game.

A half hour later, the other team admitted defeat, and Wyatt's was declared the winner. After some celebratory pats on the back, Wyatt got a drink out of a large cooler nearby and jogged back to the beach blanket. He collapsed with a groan. "Whew! That was harder than it was last year. I'm getting out of shape." He took a long drink of his Gatorade then swiped at his forehead with his arm.

Chrissy kept her gaze on the crowd so she wasn't caught staring at his bare chest. She seriously doubted the guy had ever been out of shape. Thankfully, he pulled his t-shirt back on. "Looks like you all had fun out there."

"It was a blast. I'm glad you and Bonnie had time to chat. I think you two would get along well."

"I think so, too. She's great with Gunner."

Wyatt nodded and downed the rest of his drink. "Being a nanny is her dream job. I missed having her on the team, though." He glanced around before lowering his voice. "I'm sure our parents weren't happy that she brought Gunner with her."

"Oh? Why's that?"

"Because they think being a nanny is beneath her." There was no missing the sarcasm in his voice.

She hesitated, uncertain what to say. "I can't imagine why. Their daughter is lucky enough to have her dream job, and she's good at it. You'd think they'd be thrilled."

"Unfortunately, it doesn't work that way in our family." Wyatt frowned as he twisted the lid on and off the empty Gatorade bottle. His gaze shifted to Chrissy, and the troubled look on his face faded.

Chrissy searched for something to say that would change the subject. "I keep expecting to see your grandmother here somewhere."

That brought a smile to his face. "It's hard for her to get out to the beach, although she will come down for the bonfire tonight. She's probably playing poker back at the resort."

Poker? Chrissy realized she was staring in surprise when he chuckled.

"Gran not only likes to play poker, but she and several of my great-uncles and an aunt hold quite the tournament every year. Trust me, we'll hear about who won later."

She found the image of Gran playing—and

winning—at a poker game amusing. "When I'm that age, I hope to be just like her."

"We all do." Wyatt squinted at the sun that was climbing higher in the sky. "What do you say we go back to the resort, find something cold to drink, and cool off a little before the scavenger hunt?"

A trickle of sweat ran down Chrissy's back. Relaxing in the air conditioning sounded like a great idea. She nodded her agreement.

They gathered everything together and headed toward the resort.

Chrissy glanced at Wyatt, who kept his eyes on their destination. When he said it didn't work that way in his family, was he only talking about Bonnie? Or was he also referring to something more personal? Did his parents disapprove of Wyatt, too?

It seemed like the more she spent time with Wyatt, the more questions she had about him and his life.

~*~

"Okay, Brody. Put the seashell in Miss Chrissy's bag."

Wyatt watched as his young nephew carefully placed the shell with the other items they'd found so far. They'd gathered everything from a bottle cap to a flower, from the shell to a popsicle stick. Actually, there were four popsicle sticks in the bag: one for each of his nieces and nephew. They'd swung by and gotten some to eat while running around outside.

It seemed like a good idea at the time. Now all of them had colorful tracks from their wrists to their elbows.

Chrissy must have noticed the same thing. "I tried to clean them up but didn't have a lot of success."

She'd jumped right in and helped him when he'd volunteered to take all four kids—aged three to seven—on the scavenger hunt. Violet was happy to not have to go running around in the heat after her twin girls, Abby and Lily, and Brody. Lucy, ever busy taking photos, appreciated his offer to take young Ruby.

"Don't worry about it. Lucy will see it as a great photo opportunity." He lowered his voice and leaned closer. "And Violet doesn't care as long as she's not the one out here."

Chrissy frowned. "That's sad."

"Yeah, it is." Abby and Brody each took one of his hands, while Lily talked constantly about the seashell she'd found and why she thought they should include it in the bag as well. The poor kids ate up the attention at family functions because they didn't get nearly enough of it at home. Violet left them with babysitters whenever possible, and her husband worked two jobs to keep their financial troubles at bay.

Wyatt had a lot of issues with how they managed their family. But right now, he'd focus on giving them the attention they craved. Thankfully, Chrissy was keeping Ruby occupied by letting her mark off the items on their scavenger hunt list. Ruby, while only five, acted more mature than her older twin cousins.

"What are we looking for now?" Lily asked, eager to start the hunt for the next item.

"How about some seaweed?" Chrissy tucked the clipboard under one arm and relinquished their bag of goodies to Ruby's care.

Brody gave a whoop as he raced for the waves. Wyatt broke into a jog to keep up with him and make sure the boy didn't run right into the ocean. "Hold up, buddy. We all need to look for it together."

That didn't stop Brody from scouring the sand at his feet. They found some kelp five minutes later, and Brody was the first to pick it up.

Everyone took turns touching it except for Abby, who backed away from it with a disgusted look on her face.

Chrissy knelt on the sand in front of her. "You know what? I've never seen seaweed up close before. It's pretty weird looking, isn't it?" Abby nodded. "But it doesn't feel as weird as it looks. You can touch it with the tip of your finger just like this." She demonstrated the movement and soon had Abby repeating it.

Even though the disgusted look never did completely fade from his niece's face, Wyatt was proud of her for facing her fears.

His attention shifted to Chrissy. She was amazing with the kids. Not only did she seem to know exactly what to say to them, but they liked her, too. Especially Ruby, who didn't move far from Chrissy's side.

Wyatt used to imagine having a family. Ever

since the mess with Ashley, he'd been content to spend time with his nieces and nephew. He was a devoted uncle, and usually it was enough. Except for moments like this. He wondered what it would be like to go on this scavenger hunt with his family. To hear his own children laugh, watch his wife and daughter ponder over the list, and then later clean the popsicle sticky off their hands and tuck them into bed for the night.

What about Chrissy? Did she hope for a family someday? He had a hard time believing that someone who took such delight in these kids wouldn't want her own. Suddenly, an image of a little girl with Chrissy's pretty hair and his eyes came to mind.

The shock of it made him almost trip when Abby stopped right in front of him. He shoved the image away and nodded toward the clipboard. "What else do we need to collect?"

Ruby carefully put a checkmark next to seaweed and grinned with satisfaction. "That's the last one. We're done!"

The kids cheered and began to race back toward the resort, leaving Chrissy with the clipboard and bag of treasures.

Wyatt reached for the bag as they followed the kids at a brisk pace. "Here, let me carry that."

His fingers went through the loops of the bag and settled next to Chrissy's. Hers were cold from holding the seaweed earlier, and he longed to take her hand in his and warm it up. Wyatt felt her fingers shift slightly. Her steps faltered as she relinquished her hold on the bag. "Thank you."

Chrissy's words were so quiet, he nearly missed them. He watched as Ruby slowed down and grabbed Chrissy's hand again, a look of adoration in her eyes.

He couldn't fault the girl. The more time he spent with Chrissy Laughlin, the more he wished she wasn't just his fake girlfriend.

Chapter Thirteen

By the time they finished with the scavenger hunt, ate lunch, and Chrissy went to her room to change, she was exhausted. Before she knew it, she'd fallen asleep on the bed. An hour later, she woke up feeling refreshed but shocked to see how much time had passed.

Chrissy got to her feet and glanced at the time again. She and Wyatt hadn't agreed to meet anywhere at any particular time, but she was pretty sure taking an hour to change clothes was longer than he'd had in mind. Hopefully he hadn't been downstairs waiting on her.

Of course he hadn't. He was here with all of the extended family members he only saw once a year. Chances were, he'd had plenty of people to talk to and things to do.

It was silly to think he was sitting down there counting the minutes until her return.

Rolling her eyes at herself, Chrissy quickly changed into a one-piece bathing suit. She chose her favorite sundress—pastel green with yellow sunflowers all over it—and slipped it on over her suit. Next, she added a towel and a book to her bag where the sunscreen and sunhat were already tucked away.

Spending some time at the beach this afternoon sounded heavenly. She had no intention of actually going swimming in the ocean, so the sundress would be perfect. But having the swimsuit on underneath meant she was prepared for anything.

Satisfied that she was ready, she made her way downstairs. There was no sign of Wyatt anywhere in the hallway, and she was just wondering if she'd missed him when she spotted him near the large windows at the back of the main room. He was talking to Gran, who waved Chrissy over.

"My dear, I'm so glad you decided to come." Gran gave Chrissy a gentle hug. "I hope you've been enjoying yourself. The only thing that might make this resort better would be to have an open buffet available all day long." She winked.

A buffet would be awesome, but Chrissy could understand why the resort might not want to have that available for the family when it was a much smaller number of people than they would normally entertain. She imagined a lot of food would go to waste. "It's lovely here, thank you. I hope I didn't keep you waiting,

Wyatt. I somehow managed to fall asleep."

Gran patted her hand. "Good for you, honey. The sooner you realize a good nap is your friend, the better off you'll be. Besides, you're on vacation. Squeezing in a nap or two should be part of the deal."

She took in Gran's loose pants, flowery blouse, and tennis shoes. "I hear you enjoy playing a game of poker or two while you're here."

Gran laughed and put a hand to her chest. "Oh, my. Yes, I dare say I do. In fact, I should probably get back in there." She shifted her attention to Wyatt. "Your Uncle Charlie is determined to win his money back." She chuckled again and patted her gray hair to make sure it was still in place. "You take your girl down to the beach and enjoy. I'll see you both tonight." She blew them a kiss and made her departure.

Chrissy waved. So Gran played poker for money. Suddenly the image of her sitting around a table playing cards and talking about food and quilting disappeared. In its place, she imagined Gran betting hundreds of dollars, cracking walnuts, and possessing the best poker face she'd ever seen. The thought had Chrissy smiling when she turned back to find Wyatt watching her.

There was a flash of appreciation in his eyes. "You look beautiful, Chrissy."

She smoothed the skirt and willed the warmth to stay out of her cheeks. "Oh! Thank you." She took in his navy swimsuit trunks and light blue shirt. She was pretty sure the guy could look handsome in absolutely anything.

He cleared his throat, and she shifted her gaze from him to the small worn spots on the toes of her sandals.

"Are you ready to head down to the beach?"

Grateful for something else to focus on, Chrissy nodded. Only then did she notice he had a small cooler slung over one shoulder and something else in a long bag over the other. They grabbed another oversized beach blanket on their way across the deck and followed the path down to the sand.

Once on the beach, they spread the blanket out, and then Wyatt unzipped the bag he'd been carrying. Within minutes, he had a canopy set up that resembled a giant umbrella. He put stakes in at each corner to keep the breeze from blowing it over.

"That is genius." Chrissy set her bag in one of the corners. "I've never seen something like this before."

"I figured a little shade would be nice after being out in the sun all morning." He put the cooler on the other side of the blanket to help hold it down. "I've got water and lemonade in here, too, if we get thirsty."

"What time is dinner again?"

Wyatt glanced at his watch. "At six. Why is that?"

"I have every intention of staying out here for as long as possible. If I'm late to dinner, you'll know where to find me." She closed her eyes and took in the sound of the waves crashing against the sand, the laughter of children as they splashed in the water, and the ever-present calls of the sea gulls.

Yes, she could easily picture herself with a beach house where she went to vacation and maybe even lived during the off-seasons when there weren't so many tourists. The only thing that would make this better was if Mom and Emma could be there to experience it with her.

One day, they'd take a trip down here together. They might not stay at a fancy resort like this, but then where they slept wasn't all that important. It was all about the ocean and the experience.

"Penny for your thoughts."

Wyatt's voice brought Chrissy back to the present. "I was thinking about my family."

"Do you regret coming?"

"No, I don't. I was just realizing how much they'd like it here, though." She sat cross-legged on the blanket, and Wyatt joined her. "And maybe feeling a little guilty because I haven't worried about Emma as much as I thought I would." She pulled her phone out of the front pocket of her bag. "Not that I haven't checked my messages just in case."

He chuckled. "There's nothing wrong with that." He paused. "Maybe it's because you know your mom and sister are fine looking after each other."

"Maybe." Chrissy sighed. "It's always been the three of us. Is it weird that this doesn't feel normal?"

"Weird? No. I think it's amazing that you are all that close and that you're there for each other. But I also think it's okay for you to do something on your own. Something for you." He looked uncertain, as though he were afraid he might have offended her.

She nodded slowly. "I know you're right. I guess I'm always waiting. Waiting for Emma to feel better. Waiting for her medications to work. Waiting for her surgery. She was sick a lot, even when we were kids. There were a lot of things she couldn't do, and I didn't want her to feel bad or left out." A fly landed on her leg, and she shooed it away. "Now I'm waiting for her to feel better and see if she'll adjust to losing her dream job, meanwhile hoping that this change will mean she'll be healthier in the long run."

"So what have you put off for yourself that you might have focused on otherwise?"

Wyatt's question was a normal one, but it made Chrissy pause. It wasn't necessarily her job. She was never one of those women who felt like she needed a high-paying career. Honestly, she'd always thought she'd work until she got married and had a family, then she'd stay home with the kids.

When she was a teenager, she'd thought she'd have her own family by now. She never imagined she'd be in her early thirties and her only date in ages was as a guy's fake girlfriend. Wow, how had so much time passed?

~*~

Chrissy seemed to struggle to answer Wyatt's question. He watched her face as she stared out at the waves. A moment later, a look of sadness flashed in her eyes. She turned her head and focused on him. "I guess there are a lot of things I didn't realize I'd been putting off until now." She shrugged, apparently unwilling to divulge more information than that.

He totally understood why she was hesitating. It wasn't like he'd revealed a whole lot of personal things to her, either. Ashley came to mind. He should probably tell Chrissy about her, although every time he thought to do so, he was able to rationalize the fact that they weren't really in a relationship, and so it didn't matter anyway.

But his goals for the future...

"Our situations are completely different, but I know what you mean about putting things off." Wyatt was thankful that there weren't a lot of people milling about their area of the beach. The last thing he needed was for any of what he was about to say to go through the mixed-up chain of mouths and wind up being told to his parents.

Even still, he lowered his voice a little as he continued. "I started working for my dad as soon as I graduated college. I never intended to work for him this long." He paused, trying to figure out where he should begin. "We have a small stable at the country club. Our members can ride the horses at their leisure. It's always been a popular amenity. More than that, though, I've seen what interacting with the horses can do for people. When my grandfather passed some years ago, Gran was depressed and sad. Going out to the stables and riding the horses helped her through that period in her life. I see that with others, too, no matter what their ages."

Chrissy was watching him intently and nodded for him to continue.

"After understanding what interacting with horses could do for people, I decided I wanted to open my own place. I want to make Joyful Hope Stables something everyone can afford. I want to have riding lessons available, a program to help seniors, and trained therapists to provide hippotherapy for children with disabilities." He started to tell her about some of his more detailed hopes and plans for the place he could clearly see in his mind's eye.

"It truly sounds amazing, Wyatt. You could help so many people that way." Chrissy's voice sounded wistful. "So what's stopped you from doing it?"

How did he explain his situation without diving into all the inheritance mess? For someone like Chrissy, who fought for the money she needed for everyday expenses, he doubted she wanted to hear about the poor timing of money being passed down to him. "Two reasons, I guess. First, I was young and dumb. I had some money coming in some years ago that I was counting on. That didn't work out. Instead of taking initiative and starting to set aside money at that point, I kept assuming the situation would work itself out, and I would have funds the easy way."

To his surprise, there no look of pity or disgust on her face, just one of acceptance as she listened intently.

"The second problem is that my parents very much disapprove of the plan. My father sees no way that I can make a good income with a place like that and feels it's foolhardy to even try. My mother agrees with him. Honestly, I completely get where they're coming from. But they are completely focused on how I won't make a fortune from this endeavor, when I just want to keep the business running and help people."

Wyatt shifted his position on the blanket. "I know I don't need their blessing, but when I've been working in the family business for so long, things get tricky. I want this to succeed. I need it to, so I've had to wait until I've saved up enough money to do this completely on my own financially. I refuse to set myself up for needing any assistance or for my business failing and my parents having the final laugh." He groaned. "That probably all sounds ridiculous, doesn't it?"

"No, it doesn't. Maybe there were things you could've done differently years ago, but that's in the past." Chrissy looked thoughtful. "It sounds like you're approaching it all with a lot of common sense and a real plan going forward. Is your dad reacting this way because he feels threatened? I can't see how your place would take away from the sales your dad gets through the country club."

"Exactly! No, it won't affect it at all. The stables are such a small part of the country club anyway. It's not about that for my parents, though…"

"…it's all about the bottom line. It's clear your

parents have put a lot of effort into building their finances—and they're quite good at it…"

"…but life isn't all about money," Wyatt finished, thankful she understood where he was coming from. "My entire job is making sure the country club runs smoothly and that we continue to improve our profit margins. I know there will be other stresses with Joyful Hope, but they'll be worth it." He shrugged. "So yeah, I guess I wish I hadn't put off saving money or moving forward with my plans years ago. But it is what it is, and I'd like to think I've learned things along the way that'll set me up for success."

"Do you have any kind of time frame in mind?"

Wyatt again made sure to lower his voice before responding. "I'm narrowing down a location now and hope to open next summer. If everything goes smoothly."

"That's amazing. I don't know your family all that well, but it seems like your parents ought to be proud of what you're doing, not criticizing it. Just my opinion."

Her words caused a warmth to spread through his chest. Bonnie and Lucy had always thought his plan was a good one, but it was different to have Chrissy's approval. Something about it made him feel like he could accomplish anything, and that bolstered his determination to pull things together.

There was a mix of admiration and something else in her eyes as she watched him. "Isn't it crazy how much family can influence what we do?" She sighed.

"There are so many things that have limited Emma because of her health. She's always sworn that she's fine remaining single, but I think she's afraid no guy will want her after all of her issues." Her voice broke, and she cleared her throat. "Now she's lost the job she loves." Tears filled her eyes, and she blinked them away. "I don't consciously put things off, but I guess I don't think it's fair to move forward in certain areas of my life if she can't. Is that silly?" She let out a puff of air as though her confession had taken a lot out of her.

"No. It's not silly." Everything in Wyatt wanted to reach for her and pull her into a hug. He fought to maintain the distance between them. "Emma is lucky to have a sister who cares so much about her." He searched for the right words. "I'll bet she'd want you to move forward and live your life. I don't know Emma all that well, but she doesn't seem like the type of person who would want to hold anyone back."

Chrissy nodded silently. This time, a tear escaped to slide down her cheek. It stopped at her jaw, suspended, until another tear joined it, and both fell onto the fabric of her sundress below.

Wyatt couldn't just sit there. He slid over a little and then put an arm around her shoulders. When she let her head tilt to rest against his, he tightened his hold on her. The sigh she released tugged at his heart.

A breeze came through and shook the umbrella canopy just a little. He listened to the sound of the waves, and it was easy to imagine that they were the only two on a deserted island somewhere. A place where money didn't matter, Chrissy's sister didn't struggle with her health, Wyatt's parents weren't always on his back. A place where he would seriously consider dating the gorgeous woman who just placed her hand on his forearm. The warmth of her soft skin rivaled the summer sun.

Out of nowhere, a young child squealed and then began to laugh. The sound made both Chrissy and Wyatt jump. She chuckled and swiped at her cheeks before she moved away from him.

"It'd be nice to be a kid again, wouldn't it?" Wyatt swept some of her hair away from her wet cheek and tucked it behind her ear.

"Yeah, it would. Being an adult isn't all it's cracked up to be."

"No, it's not." He smiled at her. "What do you say we go for a walk along the beach and forget all of this stuff for now."

"I think that sounds like a really good idea."

Wyatt stood and offered her a hand to help her up. This wasn't a deserted island, and there were a lot of reasons why he and Chrissy would probably never work. But for now, he chose to ignore them. For now, he'd enjoy pretending to be her boyfriend.

Chapter Fourteen

Being here this weekend was supposed to be a charade, so how come it didn't feel that way? Chrissy stooped to pick up a small seashell and add it to the growing collection in a bag Wyatt carried. He'd suggested she gather them and take them home to share with Mom and Emma, which was super thoughtful of him. They'd been able to find quite a few of them so far.

They didn't exactly have the beach to themselves, but everyone was so busy having fun and enjoying the water that conversations were usually short and in passing. Chrissy saw several family members she'd met before and was happy when they waved or spoke as though she'd been going to this reunion for years.

Most of her conversation with Wyatt over the last two hours had been fun and light, which was just fine after the heavier topics they'd covered earlier.

Chrissy still couldn't believe that his parents disapproved of his plans for Joyful Hope Stables. Good grief, if her kid had goals to put something together like that to benefit so many people, she'd not only be proud, but do what she could to help. She'd have to remember to put the smile on and act normal around them later, so she didn't give a hint as to how she really felt about them.

She thought back to everything she'd told him as well. He hadn't blamed her or made her feel silly. And he'd been right about Emma and what she would say if she knew how Chrissy felt. At this point, though, Chrissy wasn't sure how to move forward or if that was even possible.

"Check this one out." Wyatt held out a small shell with some purple on it.

"Wow, that's really pretty."

He smiled and added it to the collection before continuing their stroll down the beach.

Chrissy let her gaze linger on him. Maybe this was how she moved forward. Even if he was going to be Emma's boss, it didn't mean that Chrissy would be lingering around the country club. They'd already met each other's family for the first time, and neither of them had run for the hills then, either.

Her heart started tripping over itself as she thought about the possibility.

Suddenly, a round of barking was followed by a small terrier racing across the sand to stop in front of Wyatt. It yapped several times more.

"Gizmo!" A man came running up behind the dog. From the way he was breathing, it was clear he'd been chasing it for a while. "Would you stop?"

Gizmo turned his back on his owner, walked up to Wyatt, lifted his leg, and proceeded to pee right on Wyatt's left foot.

Wyatt's jaw dropped, Gizmo's owner's face turned red, and Chrissy clamped her lips together to keep the laughter at bay.

The guy scooped the small dog into his arms with a reprimand. "Hey, man, I'm sorry about that." The guy cringed and left with the dog.

Wyatt stared at Chrissy, a serious look on his face. His gaze shifted to his foot.

Chrissy tried to stop laughing but succeeded for only a moment before she snorted. She slapped a hand over her mouth. Normally, she might be embarrassed to have made such a sound, but this was just plain too funny, and giggles started to escape.

"Right. Because my leg looks like a fire hydrant." He was still trying to maintain his composure, but one corner of his mouth lifted slightly. "I'll be right back."

She watched as he walked into the waves far enough to wash his foot off. By the time he returned, she'd managed to get her humor under control. Well, mostly. She squeezed her right hand into a fist as hard as she could to keep from laughing again.

"Well," he began, "I can honestly say that's the first time that's ever happened."

"Who was that guy?"

"I don't even know."

That was all it took. Chrissy was giggling again, and this time, Wyatt joined her. His deep laughter did funny things to her heart and warmth spread through her body. "I'm pretty sure I'll be laughing at this memory for a long, long time."

"I sure hope this isn't the only thing you're going to remember from your weekend here." It was said as a joke, but there was a measure of seriousness in his expression.

"No, it's not the only thing."

A wave came in, but Chrissy barely noticed. Wyatt was watching her face with such intensity she held her breath. He took several steps until they were nearly toe-to-toe.

"Good, I'm glad."

Her pulse picked up tempo as he leaned in and covered her lips with his. A soft sigh escaped her, and that was all Wyatt needed. His free arm went around her waist and pulled her closer as their kiss deepened.

Chrissy melted into him, only aware of the two of them and the rhythmic feel of the waves swirling around their feet.

Until something wrapped itself around her ankle.

Chrissy startled and let out a squeal followed by a little jig.

"What's wrong?"

Chrissy gripped his arms and looked down at her feet. A strand of seaweed had wound its way around her right ankle.

Her shoulders shook with silent laughter. "I'm so sorry." She allowed one arm to fall to her side. Heat burned her face, rivaled only by the lingering memory of their kiss.

Wyatt chuckled. He bent down and freed her foot before tossing the seaweed back into the ocean. His watch beeped. After a quick glance at it and the direction they'd come from, he sighed. "We'd probably better head back so we're not late for dinner. Besides, between the peeing dog and attacking seaweed, we may need to quit while we're ahead."

They both laughed. She took the hand he offered, and he threaded their fingers together before giving her hand a squeeze. Chrissy knew he was right about returning to the resort, but the last thing she wanted to do was leave the beach. Besides, she knew all too well that the magical feel of the afternoon and that amazing, toe-curling kiss was going to be replaced with reality.

She took in his profile framed by a brilliant blue sky. What if this could be her new reality? Was that even something Wyatt wanted? Hope blossomed as they walked hand in hand.

~*~

Unlike lunch and breakfast, Chrissy and Wyatt ended up sitting at the same dinner table as his parents, Violet, and three other family members. Truthfully,

Wyatt had hoped to avoid this situation for the duration of the trip but knew that it was highly unlikely.

While breakfast and lunch had been served buffet style, dinner was a much fancier occasion. They'd already been served soup and salad and were waiting for the main course to be brought to the tables.

Wyatt rested his left arm across the back of Chrissy's chair and softly brushed her shoulder with his thumb. He didn't do it just because he wanted to maintain a point of contact with her, although that was certainly the primary reason. He also hoped to remind the others at the table that she was with him, and as such, he expected them to behave themselves. So far, conversation had mainly centered around a trip an uncle took to Paris and how his mom intended to mirror that trip in the next year or two. Honestly, Wyatt had started to tune the topic out.

Instead, he kept thinking back on his time on the beach with Chrissy. It'd been one of the best afternoons he'd ever had. Then to end it with that kiss…

At the time, he'd known he shouldn't kiss her again. It didn't matter how much his brain tried to remind him of that, nothing short of a tidal wave could've stopped him. He'd been pulled toward her with a force he couldn't explain. That kiss was sweet, but when she sighed and kissed him back, it was even more amazing.

Wyatt could've gone on kissing her forever. He'd sure rather be doing that now instead of listening to details about Paris. This weekend was going by way too fast. They'd be headed back to Clearwater by nine tomorrow morning.

Was there even a possibility that some of the magic from their trip could follow them back? If he kissed Chrissy goodbye when he took her home and asked her out on a real date, would she object? It was a gamble, but the more he spent time with Chrissy, the more he thought it would be worth it to take the risk.

Something his father said broke through his thoughts and jerked Wyatt right back to the conversation at hand. "I'm sorry, what was that?"

Violet flashed him an annoyed look, the corner of Mom's mouth pulled to the side like it did when she disapproved of something, and Dad only pierced him with that no-nonsense glare of his.

"I was saying that if I did take your mother to Paris next fall, I'm sure my son would have no trouble overseeing the family businesses while we were gone."

Next fall? Wyatt had every intention of having Joyful Hope up and running by then. While he was sure he could look in on a few things for them, running all the many businesses was not something he'd be able to do. A new company—no matter what the goal—was like a campfire. It had to be tended to, protected, and constantly stoked to keep it going.

This wasn't the time or the place to talk about that, though. Instead, he swallowed back what he really wanted to say. "I'm sure we can discuss all of that sometime next spring."

That should've placated them for the time being, but Violet smoothed her hair back as though even a strand would dare be out of place. "Maybe he's finally going to open up that ridiculous charity he's talked about for years." Her voice dripped with sarcasm.

"Of course he's not." Mom patted her lips with her napkin. "He wouldn't start up a new hobby while we were out of the country."

Despite every effort to maintain a cool composure, Wyatt's eyebrows rose right along with his temper. Mom said this as though they hadn't just now started to consider going to Paris. And hobby? Really?

He sat up straighter and brought his arm down from Chrissy's chair. "Any plans I have for my stables were set in motion long before I heard about the possibility of this trip tonight."

Dad had just finished his salad. He set his fork across the plate, wiped his hands off on the cloth napkin he'd laid across his lap, and leaned back in his chair. "Son, you work for me. If I need you to oversee the company while I take your mother on a well-earned trip to Paris, I expect you to do so. I'd hoped you'd gotten over that silly notion of opening a charity stable by now."

Wyatt hadn't realized he'd balled his hands into fists until Chrissy covered one of his hands with her own. He forcibly relaxed and focused on the feel of her soft palm against his.

"I think Wyatt's plans are admirable," Chrissy

spoke from his side. "A place like that will help so many people."

Her praise made Wyatt's heart swell with pride. Not just because she was supporting his business idea, but because she'd spoken up for *him*.

Violet made a noise that sounded like a cross between a grunt and a laugh before addressing Chrissy. "I'm sure charity is something Chrissy is more than familiar with."

Wyatt pointed a finger at her. "See here, Violet—"

His aunt sitting across the table cleared her throat loudly. "I heard a rumor that Gran wanted to set up a fireworks display during the bonfire this year. Was the resort not open to the idea?"

She was clearly trying to change the topic to something more neutral. Despite the expressions on Violet's and Dad's faces revealing that they'd rather continue the conversation, his aunt succeeded.

The wait staff brought in plates of steak and shrimp. This was the meal Wyatt always looked forward to each year. He couldn't fathom eating right now, though, when it felt like his stomach was filled with a lead balloon.

He tried to focus on Chrissy instead. He told her about some of the past activities they'd had at the reunion. She shared about the time, not long after Emma had started working for the vet clinic, she'd brought home a litter of eight puppies they spent all night feeding from a bottle. Wyatt was able to eat the majority of his meal to the accompaniment of Chrissy's beautiful laughter.

Dessert was served, although many people opted out in favor of s'mores around the bonfire. Wyatt suggested they do the same and was relieved when Chrissy quickly agreed. They excused themselves and escaped from the dining room.

He looked down at his slacks and nice button-up shirt. They'd changed clothes before dinner, knowing that it would be a fancier affair. "I think I'm going to change again before we go out to the bonfire. This feels entirely too stuffy for campfire smoke and s'mores."

Chrissy giggled. "I have to say I agree." She motioned to the pretty dress that flowed to her calves. "Shorts and a t-shirt seem like a much better outfit for that kind of event."

The pastel blue fabric of her dress fit her perfectly. She was pretty no matter what she wore, but Wyatt had to admit that her choice of dresses was becoming one of his favorites. He was pretty sure the sundress she wore on the beach earlier that afternoon would forever be associated with ocean waves and sweet kisses.

They took the elevator upstairs and walked down the hall to pause in front of Chrissy's room. Wyatt took her hand in his. "I'll meet you in fifteen minutes?"

She gave a little nod. He kissed her hand and waited for her to disappear into her room before going into his.

Suggesting they go out together for real was going to be a gamble. But if how he felt now was any indication, Wyatt didn't think he could go back to only running into Chrissy at the coffee shop after this.

For the first time in more years than he'd care to count, Wyatt finally allowed himself to hope for the family he'd always wanted.

Chapter Fifteen

Chrissy held a graham cracker with a piece of chocolate out for Wyatt. He put the roasted marshmallow over it, and then she used the other piece of cracker to slide the marshmallow off the stick, sandwiching it all together in layered gooey goodness. "Do you want this one?" She offered it to Wyatt.

He shook his head. "Go for it, I'll roast another."

"Okay. I'll get the rest of it ready for you when you bring it back."

He flashed her a grin.

Chrissy relaxed in one of the two chairs they'd claimed. They were close enough to the bonfire to enjoy the experience, but far enough away that it wasn't too hot. She could see Wyatt against the dancing red and orange flames, although the sun would be setting soon.

She bit into her s'more and released a contented sigh. This was a fabulous way to end the day. Dinner aside, it'd been nearly perfect. Sure, watching the volleyball game and helping the kids had been a lot of fun. Spending time on the beach searching for seashells and chasing the waves had been amazing. She would've enjoyed all of that if it'd been just her.

What made it all special, though, was experiencing it with Wyatt. When she'd first decided to pose as his girlfriend for this reunion, she'd been sure it would be a mistake. She'd have to thank Mom and Emma for encouraging her to go and Wyatt for being so convincing when he insisted she would enjoy it.

It'd be difficult to go back to real life again tomorrow. Would he still come by the coffee shop as often as he had before? If Emma started working at the country club, would Wyatt mind if Chrissy swung by once in a while to say hello to both of them?

She couldn't imagine going back to being just friends or whatever it was they were before this weekend.

Wyatt returned with his roasted marshmallow. She rushed to put together the graham crackers and chocolate for him then laughed when he took a bite and had melted marshmallow stringing from his mouth to his hand.

He licked his fingers and chuckled. "Classy."

That had her laughing harder as she finished her own treat and tried to wipe away the sticky residue on her hands. "They're almost too messy to be worthwhile, aren't they?"

"Bite your tongue, woman. S'mores are always worthwhile." He waggled his eyebrows and finished the rest of his in one bite. "Although, I do think one will be enough for tonight."

Chrissy agreed. Despite the tense atmosphere at dinner, she'd still managed to eat more than she normally did. There was no way she was going to let any of that shrimp go to waste. And the steak? It'd been amazing. She'd wished she could've wrapped up the leftovers and taken them home.

Wyatt sank into the chair beside her and reached for her hand.

Yeah, she could easily get used to this.

Gran approached from one side, a large cane in her right hand, with Lucy holding on to her left arm. She used the bottom of the cane to tap Wyatt's foot. "I hope you are both stuffing yourselves silly."

They smiled, and he nodded. "We did. Have you roasted marshmallows yet, Gran?"

She tilted her head toward Lucy. "That's what we're about to do now. It's a lovely evening for a bonfire, don't you think?" She looked up at the sky.

Chrissy's gaze followed, and she marveled at how she could already see some of the brightest stars in the darkening sky. "So who won the poker game this afternoon?"

"Let's just say there are some individuals, who will remain nameless, that are already insisting on a rematch next year to make some of their money back."

Gran gave her a wink. "You two young people enjoy the evening."

Lucy gave them a wave and continued to escort Gran to a spot on the other side of the bonfire. Chrissy watched Gran unfold her cane into a chair that she eased herself into. "Your grandmother is a seriously amazing lady."

"She really is." He squeezed her hand. "I don't know about you, but that s'more made me thirsty. I think there are drinks up at the patio. Can I grab you something?"

"A bottle of water would be great, thank you." Between the sweet dessert and the warmth from the bonfire, her throat was parched.

"You're welcome. I'll be back in a few minutes. Save my seat?"

"Absolutely."

Wyatt stood and then bent to place a kiss on her cheek near her ear before disappearing into the darkness behind her.

Chrissy touched her cheek and sighed contentedly.

She was staring at the bonfire and admiring the way the flames danced in the breeze when someone sat in Wyatt's chair. She was turning to tell the person the seat was already taken when she realized it was Violet. Fantastic. Apparently, she was in the habit of nabbing newly-vacated chairs. If the sour look on the woman's face was any indication, she hadn't stopped for a friendly chat.

"I see you and my brother are having fun together."

"I'm having a great time. Wyatt's the sweetest guy I've ever met." Truth.

"Yeah." Violet's tone insinuated she didn't entirely agree. "Ignorance is bliss, after all."

What was that supposed to mean? The last thing Chrissy wanted to do was encourage Violet. But either there was something on her face that showed her curiosity, or Violet was going to tell her anyway, because clearly she wasn't going to just let things be.

"You should know that Wyatt was engaged once."

Chrissy kept her focus on the bonfire and tried not to react. He'd been engaged? When?

"He and Ashley were the perfect couple. They were suited to each other, had the same goals and interests. I think they would've been happy if..." Violet's voice trailed off.

Clearly Chrissy was being baited. Violet wanted to tell her the whole story, but she wanted Chrissy to ask to hear it. Chrissy didn't trust Violet any further than she could throw her, yet she couldn't help but wonder why Wyatt had never told her about his engagement with Ashley. How long ago had that been?

Violet sighed, obviously displeased with Chrissy's lack of interest. "Once poor Ashley found out my brother was only marrying her to get access to our father's money, it was over. Ashley and I have been friends since grade school, and I've never seen her more devastated than she was that day."

There was no way. Wyatt would never use someone like that. Chrissy leveled Violet with a look of warning and tried to ignore the way her stomach clenched. "I don't believe it."

"You should. Our parents refuse to hand Wyatt his inheritance until he's married and settled down. If there's one thing he cares about more than anything else, it's that stupid charity of his. He'd do anything to get that money and put his plans into motion, including marrying someone he doesn't love." The look Violet gave her was one of pity. "You're just the next Ashley, and I want to spare you the grief and embarrassment of letting this *relationship* go on any further. I'm so sorry you had to find out this way, Chrissy." Her use of the word relationship was filled with loathing.

Part of Chrissy wanted to slap Violet for what she was insinuating. But another part of her wondered why Wyatt had never told her that he and Ashley were engaged. Was he trying to hide it? Surely he hadn't tried to marry the woman strictly for his inheritance. He'd told her that he'd been expecting some money to come in, and when it didn't, it pushed his plans back. Was this what he was talking about? She couldn't imagine him doing something like that. She scanned the crowd around her for Wyatt's face and didn't see him anywhere in the fading daylight.

"Look, the reason I'm telling you all of this is because Ashley's here. She told me she's come to terms with the relationship she had with Wyatt, and she still wants to marry him." Violet relaxed in the chair, a smug look on her face. "She always was suited to our lifestyle. And you're…not."

Tears pricked the back of her eyelids, but Chrissy refused to let them fall. All she wanted was for Violet to go away and leave her alone. Again, she searched for a sign of Wyatt and finally spotted him. To her surprise, a woman was holding onto his arm as though she were hanging onto his every word. Chrissy wished she could see their faces, but what dwindling daylight remained wasn't bright enough for that.

Violet sat up straighter and smiled. "Oh, good! Ashley found him." She had the nerve to pat Chrissy's shoulder. "I'll be happy to take you over and introduce you to her if you'd like."

The tears she'd been holding back were past the point of containment. She wouldn't give Violet the satisfaction of crying in front of her. "No. It's actually getting late, and we need to drive back to Clearwater early tomorrow. I think I'm going to head to my room."

"All right. I'll let Wyatt know. Good night, Chrissy." With that, Violet stood and walked away.

Chrissy sniffed and swiped at a tear that had escaped. How could she have been so stupid? She'd told herself when she came here that this was all an act. She'd known that she and Wyatt were far too different for anything to work between them. Then she'd allowed one amazing day to convince her that maybe, just maybe, she'd been wrong.

Her vision blurry, Chrissy picked her way through the crowd, avoided Wyatt and Ashley, and made her way back to the resort and her room. When she finally collapsed on the bed, the tears flowed freely.

~*~

Wyatt could barely contain his disgust the moment Ashley latched herself on his arm. What was she doing here? She wasn't family, and he certainly hadn't invited her.

"It's SO good to see you, Wyatt." She squeezed his arm in a hug and then didn't let go. "It seems like forever. When Violet invited me to come for the bonfire and told me you'd be here, I jumped at the chance." Her voice couldn't be any more sugarcoated. "So what have you been up to?"

"Relaxing, visiting, enjoying the food." He tried to pry his arm out of her grip, but she managed to exchange one of his arms for the other. "Have you run into Violet yet? I'm sure she'd be excited to see you. Maybe if you looked for her inside?"

Ashley sighed contentedly. "Oh, I found her earlier. She's the one who told me you were heading to the deck. Maybe we should grab something cold to drink and visit for a while. I heard there's an open bar inside."

"I don't drink." He wanted to tell her he wouldn't sit down and drink a glass of water with her, either. There was next to nothing she could say that would convince him to spend time with her. "Look, someone's waiting for me." He held up the two bottles of water he held for emphasis.

Either Wyatt's hint went completely over her head, or she chose to ignore it. Either way, she attempted to turn him back around toward the resort. That's when he decided he was going to have to be more forceful. He removed her arms from his and took a step back. "If Violet invited you, you should probably go find her. My girlfriend is waiting for me."

Without glancing behind him, Wyatt strode down the pathway and across the sand back to where the large bonfire continued to burn. He reached their chairs. Not only was Chrissy nowhere to be seen, but they'd been claimed by someone else.

He searched around the bonfire and even asked Gran if she'd seen Chrissy. No one seemed to have noticed where she went.

The attempt to call her went directly to voicemail. It was so loud outside, she probably wouldn't be able to hear her phone ring anyway.

Stamping down his frustration, he decided to head back to the deck in case she'd gone to find him. He was stopped by family members three times before he even made it there. He again tried to call her with the same result.

What was he supposed to do now? Worry morphed into dread when he saw Violet approaching him. "Are you looking for Chrissy?"

"Yes. Do you know where she is?"

"I'm pretty sure she went back inside." Violet cringed dramatically. "I think she may have seen you and Ashley. She seemed pretty upset."

"What did you tell her?" His voice came out deeper and harsher than he'd intended, but it had the desired result.

Violet flinched before pasting on her well-rehearsed wounded expression. "I have no idea what you're talking about. I'd like to think Chrissy's smart enough to draw her own conclusions." She raised her eyebrows, turned, and disappeared into the darkness outside.

Wyatt frantically searched the main area and dining room, excusing himself twice when someone came up to visit with him. He jogged to the elevator and took it up to their floor. When he got to Chrissy's room, he paused before knocking on the door. Nothing. He knocked again. "Chrissy, if you're there, we need to talk."

Only silence answered. He looked at the bottom of the door and noted that there no visible lights on inside. It was after eleven. If she had been upset, maybe she'd gone to bed.

There wasn't a thing he could do if he couldn't find her or get her to answer the door.

He finally went to his own room and kicked off his shoes before collapsing on the small couch. He pulled his phone out and sent Chrissy a text.

"I couldn't find you. I hope everything's okay. I checked your room, but you didn't answer. We need to talk before we head home tomorrow. Call me, okay?"

That was all Wyatt could do. He stayed awake for some time, hoping his phone would ring or that he'd get a text. It was after two in the morning before Wyatt finally fell into a fitful sleep.

Chapter Sixteen

Chrissy's eyes ached when she woke up the next morning after crying her heart out the night before. Now she had a three-hour car ride with Wyatt to look forward to. At least she'd have Bonnie and little Gunner there as a buffer. If she and Wyatt could avoid any serious conversations for the duration of their trip home, that would be best. Chrissy couldn't guarantee she wouldn't start crying again, and that was the last thing she needed to do in front of him.

She was supposed to *pretend* to be his girlfriend. Crying over the guy was not only ridiculous, but he'd probably think she was being overly emotional and clingy.

Chrissy sighed. It'd taken about everything she had to ignore his knock on the door last night and the texts he'd sent. She would've turned her phone off completely except she needed to keep it on in case Mom or Emma needed her.

As much as she might like to, she couldn't put the day off any longer. Chrissy dragged herself out of bed, took a shower, and repacked her things. She and Wyatt had agreed to head back at nine, and she managed to make it downstairs with only ten minutes to spare. She handed her luggage over to one of the employees who promised it would be loaded into Wyatt's car when they brought it around.

There was no sign of Wyatt. She wandered to the patio door and stepped out on the deck. The numerous topiaries made it a little difficult to scan the deck effectively. She was just about to head in again when hearing someone mention her name made her stop.

The voices were coming from the other side of one of the topiaries. She remembered from yesterday that there was a wooden bench nestled there against the railing. Chrissy held her breath and tried to figure out who was talking.

"I don't know what came over Wyatt inviting that gal like he did. She had no place here."

Chrissy was almost sure that was Mrs. Tabor.

"She most certainly did not."

As soon as she heard the man's voice, she knew it was Wyatt's father. She shouldn't listen in on his parents' conversation, but knowing they were talking about her meant she couldn't quite walk away. No one else was close by since most people were either eating breakfast inside or getting ready to leave.

Mrs. Tabor clicked her tongue. "You'd think he would've learned his lesson before. He should've married Ashley. She certainly would've put a stop to this ridiculous charity he's so obsessed with."

"One thing is for certain." There was some shuffling. "If Wyatt doesn't come to his senses soon, he'll see none of that money. I expect him to commit to the family business, and I expect him to marry someone who isn't looking for a handout."

His words drove a stake straight into Chrissy's heart. She bit her bottom lip to keep quiet. More shuffling told her they were leaving the bench. Her throat tightened as she pushed on the door and went back into the resort. She needed to get as far away from this place—and these people—as she could.

Just when she was starting to feel like the walls were closing in on her, she noticed Wyatt visiting with some people. He quickly excused himself and strode in her direction.

"Hey. I was getting worried about you." He cupped her elbow with one hand. "I didn't invite Ashley—"

"Let me guess: Your parents did."

"Actually, it was Violet. She—"

"Oh, good! I didn't miss you guys." Bonnie approached with Gunner on her hip. "Teething makes it rough on sleep. I sure hope we didn't keep our neighbors awake." She stifled a yawn. "Thanks for letting me go back with you. Gunner's dad is supposed to be home right after lunch, and I could use the afternoon to chill before going back to caring for this little guy again tomorrow morning."

Chrissy tried to ignore the feel of his hand on her elbow. It dropped away moments later when he offered to take Bonnie's diaper bag. He turned to take Chrissy's small handbag as well, but she shook her head. "I appreciate it, but you've already got your hands full."

Grudgingly, he led the way toward the front of the lobby. Moments later, one of the doormen had his car brought around and all of their luggage loaded in the trunk. Someone else got the baby's car seat strapped into the back where Bonnie secured Gunner and then sat beside him. That left Chrissy with the passenger side in the front. Wyatt waited for her to get in before closing the door behind her.

The drive home was weird and awkward. Bonnie carried on the conversation about family members who looked different from last year, who didn't come, and all the news she'd heard. Wyatt chimed in, although he kept casting concerned glances Chrissy's way.

Chrissy knew not talking at all would be worse, so she asked for clarification about who different people were and commented when she could. For the most part, she rode in silence and listened to the siblings chat.

At one point, Gunner fell asleep. Not surprisingly, Bonnie joined him shortly afterward with her head leaning against the window.

Wyatt reached over and placed a hand over hers. "We need to talk."

"Not now." Chrissy removed her hand under the guise of having to fix the strap of her seatbelt and then straighten her hair. The last thing they needed was for Bonnie to hear any conversation they had. Besides, she didn't even know where to begin. It was bad enough that he might have been engaged before and didn't tell her. But if he really was trying to marry someone to get access to the money his parents had promised him...

There was part of her that wondered if Violet hadn't just made up the whole story. Chrissy certainly wouldn't have put it past her, and if she hadn't heard something similar from Mr. and Mrs. Tabor, she might have been inclined to think that.

As far as Chrissy was concerned, the best-case scenario was that Violet had been lying, and any relationship Wyatt might have with Chrissy would result in his parents refusing to give him the money he needed to start Joyful Hope. That would make it even easier to cut ties. His dream was worth fighting for, and she wasn't about to jeopardize his chances at succeeding.

No, it didn't matter what he told her or what the truth might be. She had to walk away, and it was as much for Wyatt as it was for herself. They weren't boyfriend and girlfriend. It ought to be as simple as a handshake and a thank you. The weekend had been wonderful up until last night, but now it was time to face the fact that real life was calling her back.

Chrissy's stomach ached and her heart hurt. She just wanted to be home again.

~*~

Wyatt was losing her, he could feel it. It was as though everything they had together had been left on that beach, and the further they drove, the smaller any chance he had with her became. He wanted to talk to Chrissy and find out what Violet said, although he could certainly imagine. He knew he should've told her about Ashley before any of this happened. He resisted the temptation to pound the steering wheel with the palm of his hand.

He may have ruined everything with Chrissy before they'd even had a chance. He just had to get her to talk to him and let him explain.

Wyatt wished he could drop Bonnie and Gunner off first, but it made no sense. He'd have to go all the way across Clearwater, past Chrissy's home, back again, and then back a third time to where he lived. It'd be obvious what he was doing, and he seriously doubted Chrissy would agree with his plans.

Gunner woke up not long after and fussed for the rest of the drive, effectively ending any chance at conversation. By the time they got to Chrissy's home, Wyatt's ears were ringing, and he knew poor Bonnie was beside herself trying to calm the baby down.

He pulled up in front of her house, put the vehicle in park, and went to the trunk to retrieve

Chrissy's things. They walked side by side to the front door. Before she had a chance to reach for the doorknob, Wyatt turned to her.

"We really do need to talk. Let me explain. Give me a chance to set right whatever it was that Violet told you."

She shook her head, her chin down and her eyelashes lowered. "We're too different, Wyatt."

He used his hand to gently lift her chin until her pretty eyes were on him. "Different isn't bad." They could hear Gunner crying from the car, and Wyatt was well aware of the fact that her mom and sister were probably watching through the window. "We've got something here, Chrissy. I don't want to let it slip away."

Moisture gathered in her eyes. She drew her bottom lip in between her teeth and shook her head again. "I can't. I'm sorry, Wyatt." She took a step away from him, her back pressed against the door. With one last, sorrowful look, she turned and made her escape.

His heart aching, Wyatt returned to his vehicle and glanced at Bonnie's face in the rearview mirror. Her eyes were wide, and her mouth opened for a moment like she was going to say something before closing again.

To his relief, she went back to trying to calm Gunner, not that it seemed to make much of a difference.

"We'll be back to his house in ten minutes," Wyatt assured her. He did everything he could to focus on driving and try not to think about Chrissy. Not that it worked.

A moment later, he felt Bonnie's hand on his shoulder. She gave it a squeeze. "I'm sorry, Wyatt. What happened?"

He shrugged. "What didn't? Violet. Mom and Dad. Life." He sighed. "She won't even hear me out. I'm not sure what Violet told her, so I can't even explain or defend myself."

"You should go back after you drop us off."

"I don't think so. She needs space, and maybe I do too."

"Do you really think that's a good idea?" It was clear from the tone of her voice how she felt about it. "Come on, Wyatt. You were happier this weekend than I've seen you in a long time. I may not know Chrissy all that well, but she wasn't exactly hating it either."

"Maybe. But she's made it clear how she feels now." He wasn't even sure how *he* felt right now. He certainly should've known better than to open himself up to this. His family didn't want him alone, but they only had one type of woman in mind for him. Bringing Chrissy to the reunion had opened them both up to hurt, and her to ridicule.

Bonnie squeezed his shoulder again and let her hand drop. Once at her employer's home, Bonnie unstrapped Gunner and lifted him into her arms. Apparently that's all the baby needed because, after an hour of crying, he quieted quickly. Wyatt helped her get the car seat and luggage into the house. He would've offered to give her a ride to her house since her car was at the shop, but she only lived a block away, and he knew she preferred to walk.

He gave his sister a hug at the doorway. "Be careful walking home, and have a good rest of your Sunday, okay?"

"You, too. And Wyatt?" She gave him a sad smile. "Don't give up on this, okay?"

"I'll see you later, Bon."

With a wave, he got back into his Jeep, thankful for the blessed silence that filled the cab. He decided to go home, take a shower, and then lie down for a nap. The plan might have worked, too, if his dreams weren't filled with the sound of Chrissy's laughter or the memory of their kisses.

Chapter Seventeen

Chrissy had no intention of going to work on Monday morning. She'd called the coffee shop the afternoon before and told them she was taking a sick day. After turning her alarm off, she'd climbed into bed early Sunday night. She would've been just fine sleeping the day away until Emma woke her up by sitting on the edge of the bed.

A glance at the clock told Chrissy it was much earlier than she would've liked. "What's up, Emma?"

"Mom and I didn't want to leave before one of us checked on you. Are you going to be okay?"

"Oh, sure." Her voice was thick with sleep and laced with sarcasm. She sat up partway in bed. "Are you headed to the country club?" She tried to sound as normal as she could. Emma needed the job, and Chrissy wasn't about to discourage it. The thought of

Wyatt being there, though, made her chest hurt.

Emma frowned. "I think it'd be too weird. I have another lead or two, and I thought I would check on those first today." The sisters leaned against the wall together. "I'm worried about you."

The irony wasn't lost on Chrissy. How many hours, days, and nights had she spent worrying about Emma and her health? How many times had she wished she could take away even a fraction of the pain her little sister felt? Now Emma was sitting silently, trying to offer what reassurance she could, when Chrissy wasn't sure anything was going to help.

She took a shaky breath. "I just needed some time before I have to go back to work and wonder whether he's going to walk into the coffee shop."

"I wish you'd tell us what happened."

Chrissy gave her a sad smile as a tear slipped down her cheek. "My carriage turned back into a pumpkin."

Emma leaned her head against Chrissy's with a sigh. "I'm sorry, Chris."

"Yeah, me too."

They sat in silence until Emma finally gave her another hug and crept out of the room. A moment later, before leaving for work, Mom came in long enough to give her a hug and tell her that there were donuts on the kitchen counter.

Chrissy tried to go back to sleep and finally gave up. She dragged herself out of bed, took a shower, and changed into a fresh pair of pajamas. She'd just thrown her dirty clothes in the hamper when her gaze caught on the bag of seashells Wyatt had helped her gather. She'd tossed the bag on top of her dresser last night. What was she going to do with them? She swept the bag into the top drawer and closed it before heading for the kitchen.

She'd brought her cell phone but hadn't yet turned it on. Now that Mom and Emma were out of the house, though, she didn't feel comfortable with not having a way for them to contact her.

Chrissy turned her phone back on before chucking it onto the couch. She got herself two chocolate donuts and a glass of milk, set them on the coffee table, then glared at her phone. Which would be worse: Reading or ignoring text messages Wyatt might have sent? Or to find out that he hadn't tried to contact her at all?

They never had donuts in the house. Obviously Mom had picked them up specifically to try and cheer Chrissy up. She wasn't sure it was working yet, but boy, they tasted good. She managed to ignore her phone until she'd consumed one of them. That's when she finally decided that she may as well rip off the bandage already.

There was one text. Chrissy squinted at the screen as though that would lessen the hit of seeing who it was from. Wyatt's name caused her heart to constrict.

"I'm sorry I dragged you into this mess, Chrissy. I hope you can forgive me one day."

What did he mean by that? Sorry that she was upset? Sorry that Ashley showed up and Violet spilled the beans about his previous engagement? Or sorry that he'd asked her to go as his pretend girlfriend in the first place? Tears once again clouded her eyes.

She wanted to punch the wall. Not only had she opened her heart when she'd been determined to do just the opposite, but somehow Wyatt had managed to take up residence there. She was pretty sure it was never going to be the same.

Talk about an excruciatingly long week, and it was only Wednesday. Every day since the reunion, Wyatt wrestled with himself over whether he should stop by Clearwater Coffee or not. He never did hear back from Chrissy after sending her the text. Then again, after everything that happened, he couldn't blame her. Although he still didn't know what had been said. Bonnie and Lucy knew nothing about it, and Violet was dodging his calls. That alone told him she had a guilty conscience.

Whatever Violet might have told Chrissy, it was probably only full of half-truths. He wished Chrissy would give him the opportunity to set the record straight. But first, he needed to know exactly what he was working against.

Wyatt recalled Violet bragging about her Zumba class every Wednesday evening and how it was doing wonders for her thighs. It wasn't exactly news he would've paid much attention to, but maybe Lucy or Bonnie knew where she went.

Two texts and twenty minutes later, he had the name and address of the gym Violet frequented. This gym had childcare, which meant she certainly wouldn't miss the class.

Wyatt finished his work day and headed for the gym. He didn't want the kids to have to listen to what could only be an unpleasant conversation, so he watched for Violet to arrive and waited for her to check the kids into childcare before approaching her.

His sister came around the corner and jumped a foot when she spotted Wyatt. She frowned, creases deepening between her eyes. "What are you doing here, Wyatt? I have a class in ten minutes."

"You and I need to have a discussion."

"Later." She tried to push past him.

"No. We're having it now. If you'd like me to follow you to your Zumba class, just say the word."

Violet sneered at him. She glanced around and ushered him to the café area and an empty corner table. She always had been afraid of what others might think of her, and apparently the people milling about the gym were no exception.

Wyatt leaned into the back of his chair. "What exactly did you say to Chrissy that night at the bonfire?"

She flipped her hair over her shoulder and opened her mouth to respond. Wyatt held up a hand to stop her.

"I want the truth. If I find out you lied to me, so help me…" He forced himself to unclench his fists. "Spill."

Her shoulders fell along with the corners of her mouth. "I told her that you and Ashley used to be engaged. I *may* have insinuated that she was the one who called it off and that she'd never gotten over you."

"You what?! And I suppose you made sure she saw Ashley talking to me, too, didn't you?"

Violet shrugged.

Ugh! First Chrissy had to hear about the engagement from Violet when she should have heard it from him. Then add in the lies and seeing Ashley there with him, and it was no wonder Chrissy was so upset. It bothered him that she hadn't given him the chance to explain. He glanced at his sister and the way she was avoiding his gaze. "What else?"

She sighed. "I may have insinuated that the only reason you were marrying Ashley was because you wanted our parents to hand over your inheritance." At least she had the good sense to look a little embarrassed.

"What is wrong with you? Seriously, Violet, what have I ever done to you that would make you think I deserve this kind of treatment?" She looked more shocked by his words than he'd seen her look in years. "What difference does it make to you if I fall in love with a woman who serves coffee to make a living? What is it to you if I want to help other people by opening Joyful Hope?"

Violet opened and closed her mouth several times, but no sounds came out.

Wyatt wasn't nearly done yet. "You think having money is all that's important. I'll tell you what, big sister. You got your inheritance, remember? And I don't see that it did you a lot of good." He pushed his chair back and stood, placing his hands on the table so he could lean closer to Violet. "If I so much as catch you talking to Chrissy without my being there again, this conversation will be a party in comparison to the one we're going to have."

He turned and started to walk away when Violet's voice caught up with him.

"Wyatt?"

He took a steadying breath then pivoted to face her again.

"Are you really falling in love with her?"

"I never got the chance to find out, did I?" The initial adrenaline rush at hearing what Violet told Chrissy faded and was replaced by a sadness that penetrated his heart.

He normally would've scoffed at the idea of falling for a woman after only knowing her in passing for six months and then spending only a few days together. But there was something about Chrissy that drew him to her. All he'd wanted to do since dropping her off at her house on Sunday was hear her voice and be near her.

The possibility that she might be feeling even half

as miserable as he was made him want to go and cheer her up.

Maybe their connection had been all him, but he didn't think so. She felt something for him, too. He could feel it in her touch and the way she kissed him back. More than anything, he knew the more time he spent with her, the more he realized it would never be enough.

One way or another, he'd get her to talk to him. To listen to his side of the story. At least then, if she walked away, she'd be doing it with all the right information.

~*~

Chrissy's heart skipped a beat every time she heard the bell ring above the coffee shop door. Her head would lift, and her eyes would immediately go to the customer coming inside. She tried to tell herself she was just doing her job, making sure she helped people in a timely manner.

In reality, when she saw the customer wasn't Wyatt, it felt like an invisible vice tightened around her heart just a little bit more. It'd been a ridiculously long week, and it was only Tuesday.

He'd sent her a text. She hadn't responded. What made her think he would just waltz into the coffee shop now? It didn't matter how much she rationalized it all in her head, there was a little part of her that clung to hope. Hope that took a hard hit every time it wasn't

Wyatt who walked through that door.

She managed to make it through another day at work and didn't relax until she got home. The moment she stepped into the living room, she found Emma with her hands clasped in front of her and a pleased look on her face.

"Guess what?"

"You won a lifetime supply of chocolate." Chrissy wanted to stay grumpy, but there was no keeping back the smile when her sister looked so happy.

"No. Though that would be something to celebrate." She paused for effect. "I got a job!"

Chrissy had tried to convince her to go ahead and interview for the positions open at the country club. Just because Wyatt worked there didn't mean Emma couldn't work there as well. Besides, clearly there was no longer a connection between him and Chrissy, which ought to make things easier.

Emma must have been able to sense what Chrissy was feeling. She shook her head. "It's not at the country club. There's a new gym opening in town. Remember when we used to watch America Ninja Warrior?" Chrissy nodded. "Well, this place has a bunch of those obstacles. They teach classes, have open gym, things like that. Anyway, they were hiring people to work the front desk, keep track of sign-ups for classes, and to help with billing. They hired me almost immediately!"

"That's great, Emma." Chrissy never would've

pegged her sister to work for a gym. Then again, there was a lot about the last year that reminded her to expect the unexpected. "And they are okay with you having a flexible schedule?"

"Yes, they are very supportive. I was assured it would be no big deal if I had to take a day off here and there for health reasons." Emma clasped her hands together and bit her lower lip like she did when she got nervous. "I think this is going to be a good move for me. Don't you?"

"Of course I do." Chrissy smiled. "Congratulations! Mom is going to be so excited when you tell her. We should do something to celebrate."

"Like what?"

"I don't know. Go see a movie in the theater? Order dinner and have it delivered?"

They talked about several options and finally decided to wait and see what Mom thought once she was home from work. The sisters settled onto the couch where Chrissy propped her feet up on the coffee table and stared at the clock on the wall.

"I take it you haven't seen Wyatt."

Chrissy sighed and shook her head. "It was silly of me to think that he'd keep coming by the shop and that things would go back to normal again. I'm not even sure I'd want normal." She gasped as memory after memory flooded her mind. "I miss him, Emma." Fresh tears spilled onto her cheeks. "And I'm going to put this horrible damper on our celebration tonight if I can't get myself under control."

Emma chuckled as she gave her a hug. "I'm just sorry you're so sad. I wish I could make things better. Maybe if I had won a lifetime supply of chocolate…"

Chrissy hiccuped. "Just tell me it's going to be okay, and that this will get better."

"It is, and it really will."

Chrissy took a deep breath and nodded slowly. Whoever said that a clean break was best should've warned people how much it hurt.

Emma sat up quickly and reached for a small package on the side table. "I almost forgot. This came for you today." She gave her a small smile before getting up and giving Chrissy some space.

There was no name in the upper left-hand corner, and the address wasn't familiar. Curious, she tore open one end and pulled out a CD in a paper sleeve with a folded note that read:

Chrissy,

I wanted to make sure you got a copy of the pictures from the reunion. I hope you like them and look forward to seeing you again.

Blessings,
Lucy

Chrissy stared at the disc for several moments. She was tempted to stuff it back in the padded envelope, but curiosity got the better of her. She carried it to the computer they shared and slid the CD into the drive.

The computer loaded the CD. Chrissy highlighted the folder and told the computer to display them as a slideshow.

Many of the photos were of people she either didn't know or barely recognized. Then there were pictures of the volleyball games and scavenger hunt. An image of Wyatt hitting the ball made Chrissy smile a little. Moments later, there was another picture of them with the four kids during the scavenger hunt. She hadn't even realized Lucy had been nearby at the time.

Chrissy was caught up in watching the computer flip through images until one of her and Wyatt made her pause the slideshow. They were holding hands on the beach. Chrissy was laughing at something he'd said, but it was the way he was looking at her that made her heart skip a beat.

If she were looking at an image of another couple, and the man had that same expression, she'd swear he was in love. But there's no way that was true, right?

Her heart twisted as she studied her own expression in the picture. That time on the beach with Wyatt had been incredible. It was like a fairy tale that was too good to be true, except she couldn't stop thinking about the handsome prince and the way it'd felt to be held in his arms.

Chapter Eighteen

Wyatt tied up a few loose ends Thursday afternoon. He'd already let everyone else know he was leaving early to take care of some personal things. He'd just stood from his chair when the door to his office opened and his father walked in. Wyatt suppressed a sigh.

"Hey, Dad. I was just on my way out." They shook hands. "What brings you by today?" Whatever it was, hopefully it wouldn't take long.

Dad pulled a chair out and sat down. Wyatt had no choice but to return to his own seat as well and do his best to look interested.

"I'm concerned, son. Concerned that you're not taking your position here seriously. Concerned that you're going to throw it all away for that charity you keep talking about." Dad clenched his jaw as he studied

Wyatt. "And what were you thinking bringing that coffee barista to the family reunion? I've tried to stress how important it is to set your priorities and then keep them in check. I don't understand where things went wrong."

Wyatt exhaled slowly to curb his annoyance. "Nothing went wrong, Dad. You and I have different priorities, that's all." His father looked like he was going to object, but Wyatt didn't have time for this to turn into a big production. "Joyful Hope Stables is going to happen. Period. It may take me longer than I'd like to get there, but I'm planning on officially opening next summer. When I do, I'm going to have to step away from my position with your company. I'd really like to stay on through the new year and then help train the person who will be taking over my job, but it's up to you how you want to handle that situation."

Dad's eyebrows raised, and Wyatt could practically hear the sound of his teeth cracking as Dad's jaw moved from one side to the other.

Before Dad had a chance to say anything, Wyatt continued. "As far as Chrissy goes, I originally brought her to Gran's birthday party so that, for once, you and Mom would quit hounding me about my personal life and Gran could celebrate in peace."

"And the reunion?"

"I brought her as my guest because I enjoy her company. She makes me happy, and I hope I do the same for her. As a woman I'm interested in, she had every right to be at that family reunion. You and Mom should've taken the time to get to know her instead of criticizing what she does for a living."

That seemed to surprise Dad more than the announcement about the stables. "You aren't telling me you're serious about this girl." It wasn't a question but a statement. Typical.

Wyatt didn't hesitate. "Yes, I am." The moment he said those words, he knew it was true. There was something about Chrissy that made his life better, that made him happier. It was something he had no intention of letting go of if he had anything to do about it. He rested his arms on the desk and gave his dad a look that he hoped conveyed how serious he was. "I'm heading over to speak with her this afternoon. I'm praying that, despite all you, Mom, and Violet have done to convince her otherwise, she'll give me a chance." He pushed away from his desk and stood. He didn't want to miss catching Chrissy at the coffee shop when she got off work.

Dad followed suit and pulled on his dress shirt to straighten out the wrinkles. "I hope you know that if you choose to open those stables, and pursue this woman, you'll never see a dime of your inheritance."

"You know what, Dad? I love you and Mom, and I respect you both, but I don't want your money." Wyatt walked around the desk until he was toe-to-toe with his father. "I don't need it. I'm financially stable with a strong, long-term plan for Joyful Hope. I don't know whether Chrissy's going to give me the time of day or not, but if she does, I'm a lucky guy to have someone that incredible even look my way." The more he spoke, the more a weight felt as though it were being lifted from his shoulders. "I don't need your criticism, and I don't need your doubt. What I could really use is your support."

Respect flashed in Dad's eyes before he drew himself up to his full height and pierced him with a firm look. "And you're sure about all of that?"

"Absolutely."

Dad held his hand out for Wyatt to shake. "We'll see you Saturday at dinner?"

"I'll be there."

With a single nod, Dad turned and left the office.

Wyatt released the breath he had been holding and allowed himself to sit on the surface of his desk. That was about as close to an approval as he'd ever gotten from Dad. He'd be shocked if he didn't have to deal with more repercussions from Mom and Violet, but that was probably the last he'd hear of it from his father.

Still stunned by the conversation, Wyatt rushed downstairs to his vehicle hoping he could catch Chrissy before she left for the evening. By the time he got there, she'd already exited the coffee shop and was walking down the street. He jumped out of his Jeep and jogged to meet her on the sidewalk.

The moment she spotted him, her eyes widened, and she came to a stop. "Wyatt? What are you doing here?"

"We need to talk." When she started to shake her head, he reached for her hand to stop her. "Please, hear me out. Then I won't bother you again if you want to leave."

She didn't object or pull her hand from his. Taking that as a good sign, he led her to the fountain where they'd first talked and sat facing her.

"I should have told you about Ashley." It was difficult to not react to the hurt on her face at the mention of his ex's name. "We were engaged to be married. It was years ago, and we didn't know each other all that well. She was constantly telling me how much she loved me. I thought I loved her, too. The rest of what Violet told you, however, wasn't true. I was not marrying her to get my inheritance money. At that time, my parents were still unhappy with my decision to one day open Joyful Hope Stables. Ashley agreed that it was a waste of time. My parents approved of her, but when she heard that they wouldn't give me my inheritance if I kept going forward with the stables, she became angry."

Chrissy's eyes were wide as she listened. She still hadn't pulled her hand away, and Wyatt held onto it like a lifeline as he continued.

"Ashley told me that we needed the money and that I was being selfish. That's when I realized she didn't love me. She loved the idea that I might gain an inheritance and, as my wife, so would she. It was me who broke off our engagement at that point. Ashley, my parents, and Violet were all furious and have never fully forgiven me for the decision. I doubted myself for a long time because of it. How could I have not known who Ashley really was?"

"It sounds like she was a master manipulator. Sometimes people like that are so good at what they do, even they believe it for a time." Chrissy's voice was quiet as she spoke. "Why did Violet invite her to the bonfire?"

"Because Violet thought it would be entertaining to invite her and mess with us. I'm not sure if she was hoping it would make me mad, break us up, or if she thought Ashley still had a chance." He shrugged. "I've never been able to understand her motivations." He looked at their joined hands and softly caressed the top of her thumb with his.

"This whole thing between us may have started off with you going as my fake girlfriend," he lifted his gaze to examine her face, "but that's not the way it ended. I miss you, Chrissy."

~*~

If everything he said was true, Chrissy couldn't blame him for calling off the engagement and walking far away from Ashley. In fact, after what she knew and had seen of Violet, the very fact that she and Ashley were best friends was enough to put a black mark on Ashley as it was.

He misses me. Those words were like a balm on her bruised and aching heart. She'd missed him too.

Desperately. The conversation she heard between his parents filled her head and prevented her from telling him she missed him, too. It didn't matter how she felt. They could take Ashley out of the equation, and it still didn't change the fact that his parents would refuse to give him his inheritance money if he pursued a relationship with her. The last thing she wanted to do was cause more trouble for him.

"Chrissy?"

It took everything in her to remove her hand from his. "It can't work." She tried to focus on the water in the fountain and keep her tears at bay. She was so sick of crying.

Wyatt leaned down to look at her. "Why not?" When she only shrugged in response, he put a hand on her shoulder and turned her to face him. "I know it's crazy, but I've fallen in love with you, Chrissy. It happened so fast, and so unexpectedly, that it's scary. There's something here between us, and I refuse to walk away from it. Can you look me in the eyes and tell me you don't feel it too?"

Chrissy's heart slammed into her ribs and stole her breath. Of course she felt it. That's what made all of this even harder. She jumped to her feet and took several steps away before turning to face him again. He'd followed her, concern etched into his features. "I overheard your parents talking. If you and I end up together, they will never give you your inheritance. Your dreams—everything you've been working toward—will be out of reach." She swallowed hard. "I can't be a part of that."

He shook his head, a tiny smile pulling at the corners of his lips. "My father confronted me earlier today, and I told him I would no longer work for him after the new year. I also made it clear that I didn't want his money. I've got a plan in place for the stables, and I'm financially capable of doing that on my own. I refuse to owe my parents anything. If they give me that inheritance, they'll hold it over my head for the rest of their lives." Wyatt approached her and took both of her hands in his. "Most importantly, I will not allow my parents, or anyone else, to dictate who I can and can't love."

"You're serious." Chrissy studied his face and saw the truth written in his eyes. Her breath caught.

"The way things started between us might not have been ideal, but there's nothing fake about how I feel." He lifted a hand and gently cupped her face. "You've managed to take my entire world and turn it upside down." He moved until his lips were only inches from hers. "I love you, Chrissy."

His touch, in combination with his words, turned her legs into jelly. Her heart raced as hope chased away the sadness beat by beat. The sounds of the fountain and people passing by faded away until they were the only two on Earth.

Chrissy smiled into his eyes. "I love you, too."

Wyatt grinned moments before his lips were covering hers in a kiss that had her practically melting into a puddle. She slipped her fingers into the hair at the base of his neck as he pulled her closer.

She had no idea how long they had kissed when he finally pulled away enough to look at her.

"For the record?"

Curious, Chrissy waited for him to continue.

"It's been torture not coming by the coffee shop to see you this week."

She definitely knew what he meant. Wyatt pulled her into a hug, and she kissed his cheek. "You know," she began, "if you come by, not only will you get your coffee, but you just might get a kiss thrown in."

Wyatt grinned. "Are you kidding? Get my coffee fix, and my Chrissy fix, all in one swoop? Honey, I'm there."

He kissed her again, and this time it was filled with the promise of many more to come.

Epilogue
September: One Year Later

Chrissy hugged Mom's arm as they followed the path to the sandy beach below. The two lines of people became closer with each step. When she and Wyatt had first decided on a small, intimate wedding on the beach, Chrissy wondered if she'd regret not having something larger. This was perfect, though: just family and a few close friends who could make the trip to Corpus Christi.

Mom leaned over as they walked and let her head briefly touch Chrissy's. "I can't believe my baby girl is getting married today," she said, just above a whisper.

Chrissy's eyes misted. "I'm so glad you're walking with me." She had few memories of Dad, but it still didn't seem right to not have him here. Mom had cried on the spot when Chrissy asked her to walk her down the aisle and quickly agreed.

The sand gently gave way beneath Chrissy's bare feet as they approached and began to walk down the aisle between rows of people. Raven and Heath smiled as she passed. Wyatt's parents, while reserved, had made the trip along with all three of his sisters. At the end of the aisle, Emma watched with happy tears in her eyes.

It made Chrissy happy to see them all, but it was Wyatt who had her heart doing somersaults.

He stood at the end of the line next to Pastor Donovan, watching her with a smile on his face, and looking handsome in a pair of black slacks and a button-up white shirt.

They paused when they reached the end of the aisle. Mom kissed Chrissy's cheek, transferred her hand to Wyatt's, and went to stand next to Emma.

Wyatt maneuvered them so that they were standing in front of the pastor before taking both of her hands in his. "You look beautiful, Chrissy."

Chrissy glanced down at her simple ankle-length white gown and back up at him with a smile. "Thank you. You look pretty amazing yourself."

He flashed her a grin as the ceremony began.

When it came time for Wyatt to say his vows, he held her hand and ran his thumbs over the tops of her fingers. "Chrissy, paying you to go on a pretend date with me may not have been the classiest thing I've ever done." The sounds of laughter filled the air. "But it was the smartest move I've ever made. No matter what storms might come our way, I know we're going to be fine because we'll face them together. I will love you every day of my life." He slipped the gold wedding band over Chrissy's finger.

Her heart swelled at his words, and she had to take a moment to swallow her emotions before she could speak. "Growing up, I used to imagine all the possible first dates I might have with my future husband. I have to admit that going to your grandmother's birthday party hadn't been one of them." More laughter and they both turned to smile at Gran as she waved at them. "I'm so glad that God has a better imagination than I do, and that He brought us together. Being with you makes every day better than the last, and I can't wait to spend the rest of my life walking beside you." Chrissy carefully placed his wedding band.

Pastor Donovan nodded approvingly. "Wyatt and Chrissy, we have witnessed the pledging of your love and commitment to each other. We have seen the sealing of your solemn vows of marriage by the giving and receiving of rings. It is, therefore, my joy and privilege to declare you husband and wife. What God has joined together, may no man put asunder. Wyatt, you may kiss your bride."

Wyatt rested his palms on each of her arms. Just when Chrissy thought he was going to lean in and kiss her, he glanced down at their feet. When he looked up again, she raised an eyebrow in question.

He grinned. "I'm just making sure there's no seaweed this time."

Chrissy giggled as he pulled her into his arms and kissed her thoroughly before hugging her close. "I love you, Mrs. Tabor."

"I love you, too. Always and forever."

Thank you!

I appreciate you for taking the time to read *Marrying Chrissy*. I hope you enjoyed it and will consider leaving a review on Amazon and/or Goodreads. I like hearing what you think about it, and it'll help other readers discover new books as well.

If you've liked the Brides of Clearwater books, you might enjoy the complete Love's Compass series as well.

Acknowledgments

There's a lot that goes into writing a book. Inspiration, of course, not to mention time and dedication. But then there are also the people in my life that not only encourage me to do what I love, but are there every step of the way.

Thank you, Doug, for standing by my side. I'm stronger with you, and I'm so glad we get to experience this thing called life together.

Franky, Kris, and Rachel, I appreciate you gals for taking the time to offer feedback on Chrissy's story. Your insight and suggestions were exactly what I needed to make this book better and to keep me on track as I wrote it.

There are a number of people who are instrumental in catching all the little typos that I somehow miss time and again. Steph, Mom (Suzanne), Denny, and Sandy, you ladies are amazing. Thank you for taking the time to read each of my books.

The cover of this book is perfect, and it wouldn't have come together without your amazing photography talent, Jennifer, or your design skills, Vicki. Thank you both.

My schedule changed so much while writing this book. Many thanks to Heather Hayden for fitting me in and for her fabulous editing skills. I appreciate you!

Most importantly, I'm thankful to my Heavenly Father for holding my hand during this particularly difficult season in life. I'm so glad that, no matter how things in life ebb and flow, He is always there to keep me grounded.

About the Author

Melanie D. Snitker has enjoyed writing fiction for as long as she can remember. She started out creating episodes of cartoon shows she wanted to see as a child, and her love of writing grew from there. She and her husband live in Texas with their two children, who keep their lives full of adventure, and two dogs, who add a dash of mischief to the family dynamics. In her spare time, Melanie enjoys photography, reading, crocheting, baking, and hanging out with family and friends.

http://www.melaniedsnitker.com
https://twitter.com/MelanieDSnitker
https://www.facebook.com/melaniedsnitker

Subscribe to Melanie's newsletter and receive a monthly e-mail containing recipes, information about new releases, giveaways, and more! You can find a link to sign up on her website.

Books by Melanie D. Snitker

Calming the Storm
(A Marriage of Convenience)

Love's Compass Series:
Finding Peace (Book 1)
Finding Hope (Book 2)
Finding Courage (Book 3)
Finding Faith (Book 4)
Finding Joy (Book 5)
Finding Grace (Book 6)

Life Unexpected Series:
Safe In His Arms (Book 1)
Someone to Trust (Book 2)

Welcome to Romance
Finding Forever in Romance

Brides of Clearwater Series:
Marrying Mandy (Book 1)
Marrying Raven (Book 2)
Marrying Chrissy (Book 3)

www.ingramcontent.com/pod-product-compliance
Lightning Source LLC
Chambersburg PA
CBHW020408210626
46816CB00006BB/2176